D1637149

Exciting Westerns by Jon Sharpe

		(0451)
☐	THE TRAILSMAN #19: SPOON RIVER STUD	(123875—$2.50)*
☐	THE TRAILSMAN #20: THE JUDAS KILLER	(124545—$2.50)*
☐	THE TRAILSMAN #21: THE WHISKEY GUNS	(124898—$2.50)*
☐	THE TRAILSMAN #22: BORDER ARROWS	(125207—$2.50)*
☐	THE TRAILSMAN #23: THE COMSTOCK KILLERS	(125681—$2.50)*
☐	THE TRAILSMAN #24: TWISTED NOOSE	(126203—$2.50)*
☐	THE TRAILSMAN #25: MAVERICK MAIDEN	(126858—$2.50)*
☐	THE TRAILSMAN #26: WARPAINT RIFLES	(127757—$2.50)*
☐	THE TRAILSMAN #27: BLOODY HERITAGE	(128222—$2.50)*
☐	THE TRAILSMAN #28: HOSTAGE TRAIL	(128761—$2.50)*
☐	THE TRAILSMAN #29: HIGH MOUNTAIN GUNS	(129172—$2.50)*
☐	THE TRAILSMAN #30: WHITE SAVAGE	(129725—$2.50)*
☐	THE TRAILSMAN #31: SIX-GUN SOMBREROS	(130596—$2.50)*
☐	THE TRAILSMAN #32: APACHE GOLD	(131169—$2.50)*

*Price is $2.95 in Canada

THE TRAILSMAN 37

VALLEY OF DEATH

by
Jon Sharpe

A SIGNET BOOK

NEW AMERICAN LIBRARY

PUBLISHER'S NOTE

This novel is a work of fiction. Names, characters, places, and incidents either are the product of the author's imagination or are used fictitiously, and any resemblance to actual persons, living or dead, events, or locales is entirely coincidental.

NAL BOOKS ARE AVAILABLE AT QUANTITY DISCOUNTS
WHEN USED TO PROMOTE PRODUCTS OR SERVICES.
FOR INFORMATION PLEASE WRITE TO PREMIUM MARKETING DIVISION,
NEW AMERICAN LIBRARY, 1633 BROADWAY,
NEW YORK, NEW YORK 10019.

Copyright © 1984 by Jon Sharpe

The first chapter of this book previously appeared in *The Badge,* the thirty-sixth volume in this series.

SIGNET TRADEMARK REG. U.S. PAT. OFF. AND FOREIGN COUNTRIES
REGISTERED TRADEMARK—MARCA REGISTRADA
HECHO EN CHICAGO, U.S.A.

SIGNET, SIGNET CLASSIC, MENTOR, PLUME, MERIDIAN and NAL BOOKS
are published by
New American Library,
1633 Broadway,
New York, New York 10019

First Printing, January, 1985

1 2 3 4 5 6 7 8 9

PRINTED IN THE UNITED STATES OF AMERICA

The Trailsman

Beginnings ... they bend the tree and they mark the man. Skye Fargo was born when he was eighteen. Terror was his midwife, vengeance his first cry. Killing spawned Skye Fargo, ruthless, cold-blooded murder. Out of the acrid smoke of gunpowder still hanging in the air, he rose, cried out a promise never forgotten.

The Trailsman, they began to call him, all across the West: searcher, scout, hunter, the man who could see where others only looked, his skills for hire but not his soul, the man who lived each day to the fullest, yet trailed each tomorrow. Skye Fargo, the Trailsman, the seeker who could take the wildness of a land and the wanting of a woman and make them his own.

*The Utah Territory, 1861,
just below Black Canyon,
where law and order are only words
that come at the end
of a six-gun . . .*

1

"You can't hang that man."

Judge Samuel Tolliver's long face grew red as he fastened watery-blue eyes on the big man with the chiseled face in the center of his makeshift courtroom. "Are you telling me who I can hang and who I can't hang, mister?" he roared.

"I'm saying this man is innocent and I don't expect you'd want to hang an innocent man," the big man answered calmly. His lake-blue eyes took in the frayed collar of Judge Tolliver's black frock coat, the stained lapels, and the starched collar that had long lost its stiffness. He'd seen judges like this one before, in other little makeshift courtrooms as seedy as this one—men bought, paid for, and owned. But, then, Owl Creek was a seedy little excuse for a town.

"You saying you want to testify in this here trial, mister?" he heard Judge Tolliver ask.

"Yes, sir, your honor," the big man said as he pulled his powerful, hard-muscled figure to its feet.

Judge Tolliver's long face grew more sour than usual. "Step up and speak your piece," he muttered. "You swear to tell the truth and nothin' else?"

"I swear," the big man said as he stepped forward.

"You've got a name? Let's have it," the judge barked.

"Fargo," the man with the lake-blue eyes said. "Skye Fargo."

He saw Judge Tolliver's eyes narrow as he exchanged glances with a thickset man in the first row of chairs, wearing a sheriff's badge on his shirt. The judge brought his eyes back to Fargo. "Heard the name," he commented. "You the one they call the Trailsman?" Fargo nodded. "What are you doing in these parts?" the judge asked.

"Passing through," Fargo said. "I saw that barn on fire last night, heard the horses screaming inside. I rode down to try to do something, but the fire was too big by the time I got there."

"So you saw the fire. That doesn't mean Tom Hanford didn't set it like Sheriff Curry says he did," the judge snapped.

Fargo's quiet calm stayed unruffled. "The sheriff says he did it alone, that he had a grudge against this man Lansing. I saw four men hightailing it away from the fire. That man wasn't one of them," he said, nodding toward the small, slightly round-shouldered man seated beside a sheriff's deputy.

"Maybe you saw wrong," Judge Tolliver said, his long face dyspeptic.

"Maybe you hear wrong," Fargo returned coldly. "Four men. Four," he repeated.

Again, Judge Tolliver's watery eyes exchanged a glance with the sheriff before returning to the big man before him. "All right, mister, you've said your piece. I call a fifteen-minute recess in this here trial."

He rose, frayed black frock coattails flapping behind him as he hurried into an adjoining room and pulled the door closed after him. Fargo returned to his seat and saw the sheriff rise and start to push his way through the spectators. The man's eyes, hard gray, paused for a moment on the big man with the handsome, chiseled face, and then he hurried out. Sheriff Curry was a bigger man than he appeared sitting down, Fargo noted, heavy, barrel chest and a thick neck, a block face with small features; short nose, tight mouth, and squinty eyes. Fargo's eyes moved across the crowded little room to halt at the girl across the way from him. Hands clenched in her lap, shoulders held stiffly pulled back, she looked taut as steel wire, but fresh and pretty at the same time.

Fargo released a long sigh. He'd come upon her only twenty-four hours ago and here he was in this dreary little courtroom. His silent snort was a derisive comment. Doing good deeds was like chasing tumbleweed: you never knew where it'd take you. Only damn fools bothered to do either. But then everybody has to be a damn fool once in a while, he smiled inwardly. The little courtroom hummed with the murmur of conversation and Fargo let his eyes half-close, his thoughts wind backward.

It had been almost noon, the sun high, as he edged his Ovaro along a ridge thick with black oak and paper birch. He'd seen the three men and the girl ride into sight through the trees, moving along open land a dozen yards below where he rode. The girl's voice drifted up to him clearly, words of anger and accusation. "You won't get away with it, damn you," she said, and Fargo reined up to peer through the trees. She had short-cut brown hair, a little turned-up nose, and a wide mouth that combined to give her a pugnacious kind of prettiness. He was too far away to see the color of her eyes, but he could see round, high breasts that filled the off-white shirt she wore. As he watched, the three men drew to a halt.

"Get off the horse, bitch," he heard one rasp, and saw a deputy sheriff's badge on his buckskin jacket. "Roy said to teach you a lesson, and we're gonna do it here and now."

"Roy Curry's a rotten, no-good bastard and you're no better. You leave me alone," the girl flung back. She started to spur the horse on, but one of the men moved in quickly and caught the animal by the cheek strap. Fargo watched the other two dismount and reach for the girl. She kicked out, and one, a long, thin, spidery man ducked away from a boot that grazed his face.

"Goddamn," he swore as he picked himself up from the ground. The girl tried to back the horse free, but the third man kept his grip. She turned as another of the men reached for her and she kicked out again. But the spidery-legged one had come around the other side and Fargo saw him grasp one of her legs and yank hard. She flew from the saddle and he grabbed her as the one with the badge came around to help him.

"Bastards," the girl shouted as she struggled, but they kept their grip and dragged her around to the other side of the horse.

"Tie her to that sapling over there," the deputy sheriff ordered, and Fargo continued to watch as the girl, cursing and kicking, was dragged and tied to the young tree, her arms stretched around the trunk so that her face pressed against the bark.

"Roy said to see you didn't come back making trouble again," the one with the badge snarled as he took a bullwhip from his saddle.

Fargo grimaced as he edged the Ovaro down through the trees. He didn't know what this was all about and he didn't like interfering in things he didn't know about. But he didn't much like what he was seeing, either, and he steered the Ovaro down the sharp slope.

"Lift that shirt up," the deputy called, and the spidery-legged man yanked the girl's shirt up half over her head. Fargo saw a tanned, young, firm-skinned, strong back and the lovely edge of one high breast. The man snapped the bullwhip as he laughed. "You're gonna be sorry you always been so goddamn high and mighty with me, honey. I'm gonna enjoy whipping your butt," he said.

Fargo moved the Ovaro into the open while the three men still had their backs to him, intent on what they were going to do. The man with the bullwhip raised his arm to send the whip lashing out. "Hold it right there, mister," Fargo said quietly, and the trio whirled in surprise. The one holding the bullwhip kept his arm upraised.

"Who the hell are you?" He frowned.

"Doesn't matter. Just drop the whip," Fargo said.

The man's mouth curled into a snarling sneer. "You come to rescue the little lady, cowboy?" he asked.

"Guess so," Fargo said.

"Well, you can guess again. You've got three seconds to get your dumb ass out of my sight," the man snarled.

"Untie the girl," Fargo said calmly.

The man's frown deepened. "Maybe you didn't hear me, cowboy," he said.

"I heard you. Untie the girl," Fargo answered.

"There are three of us here. You crazy?" the man said.

"Either that or maybe I can't count," Fargo said softly. He smiled inwardly as he saw the three men glance at each other. He knew what they were thinking; no man took on three guns unless he was damn sure of himself or a damn fool, and they didn't see a damn fool in the ice-blue of his eyes. Fargo saw the deputy's wrist go backward, his shoulder tighten as he started to send the bullwhip lashing out. Fargo's hand moved and the big Colt .45 seemed to fly from its holster and fire all in one motion. The shot creased the man's hand and he roared in pain as the bullwhip flew from his grasp.

"Jesus," he said as he half-turned and pressed the side of his hand to his shirt.

Fargo's eyes flicked to the other two men. He saw the spidery-legged one swallow hard as the third one remained motionless. "Mount up and move out," Fargo said.

The deputy spit back angry words as he tied a kerchief around his hand. "I see you again, I'll put daylight through you," he said with a bravado not echoed in his eyes. "Besides, you're interfering with official business. She's my prisoner."

"He's a damn liar. I'm nobody's prisoner," the girl called out.

"I got orders to see she didn't come back to town," the man said.

"You just got new orders. Get your ass out of here," Fargo said.

The man started to pull himself on his horse, the other two following. "We've a score to settle, mister," the deputy growled.

"Whenever you want," Fargo said. "Order yourself a pine box first."

The man glared and turned his horse away to ride off at a fast trot with his two companions.

Fargo watched till he was satisfied they weren't returning, and then strode to the girl. She wriggled her torso and the shirt tumbled down as he reached her. He untied her wrist bonds and saw her eyes search his face, take in the chiseled handsomeness, the black brows. Light-brown, round eyes, he noted. They were wide, frank, and they fit the pugnacious prettiness of her.

"I owe you," she said. "That bullwhip would've cut me up real bad. I'm Bess Hanford."

"Fargo . . . Skye Fargo," the Trailsman replied. "What was that all about?"

"My pa," she snapped angrily. "He's in Sheriff Curry's jail for burning down Dorrance Lansing's barn and killing three horses." Her eyes flashed brown flame. "It's a lie, of course, one more piece of railroading. Only worse. My pa won't give in like the others."

"The others?" Fargo inquired as he walked beside her to her horse, a solid brown mare with a hint of Morgan in her, he noted.

"My pa's not the first. But it was only a matter of time before Dorrance Lansing got to us. He's cleared most everybody out of the valley," Bess Hanford said, and her voice was suddenly flat and filled with dejection, her pretty face turned dark and grave. She halted beside her horse, and her light-brown eyes studied him again. "It takes some telling. If you've a mind to hear, come with me. I'll fix you a good supper while we talk," she offered.

"Why not?" He shrugged. A good meal and a pretty girl were a lot better than beef jerky and wandering coyotes. He'd come near Owl Creek following a lead that hadn't held up. But then most of them didn't. Yet he never turned away from any. He couldn't, any more than a starving man can turn away from food. That day when they'd murdered his family was written in the blood. It would be erased only when he'd caught the last two of the murdering gang. They were out there, a debt waiting to be collected. Someplace, somewhere, sometime, he'd find them, just as he had the others.

He turned and pulled himself onto the Ovaro as Bess Hanford rode off. She had a round little rear that filled the riding britches and she rode with a good, steady hand, he saw. They'd gone but a mile or so into a long, lush valley when she turned and led the way to a small house with a stable and hog pens to one side. Fargo saw at least twenty hogs in clean pens and, behind them, rows of tilled soil. He followed Bess into the stable and unsaddled the Ovaro. "Got good pork chops waiting for tonight, best you'll ever taste," she told him pridefully.

"Must be your own stock," he grinned, and she nodded as she led him into the house. A wide and spacious room made the house seem larger than it had from outside. A long, worn green sofa rested on a frayed rug, and the room opened onto a kitchen with an open space between that was hung with kettles and iron skillets. Bess gestured to the long green sofa as she opened a corner cabinet and brought out a burlap-covered jug.

"Good sippin' whiskey," she said as she poured a glass for him and one for herself. "Sit down while I set the fire to burning," she said, and he folded his long frame onto the sofa and took a slow pull on the whiskey. She'd been right, he murmured. It was good, full-bodied rye. His eyes watched her as she came back into the room. No sensuous gliding walk for Bess Hanford, he observed: she moved with quick, energetic, bouncy steps that made her jiggle in all the right places. She slid down beside him and her pert face grew solemn at once as she sipped the whiskey. "About Dorrance Lansing," she began. "He wants the land in this valley and he's rich enough to do anything to get it. He's behind everything that's happened."

"Just what's that?" Fargo asked.

"Almost everyone in the valley has been framed by Dorrance Lansing and cheated out of their lands. He uses a jackal of a sheriff and a hyena of a judge."

"How do they frame people?" Fargo questioned.

"They see that someone gets into an argument with Lansing or one of his men. Next thing, something happens and they frame one of the valley people for it, the way they've framed my pa for burning down Lansing's barn," Bess said, and took a long pull of the whiskey. "They'll give him the same choice they gave the others, hanging or clearing out, leaving their land."

"For this Dorrance Lansing to pick up," Fargo said.

"Exactly," Bess Hanford bit out. "Naturally, clearing out is better than hanging to most people."

"Most?" Fargo frowned.

"Bill Stebbins wouldn't give in. I always felt he thought they'd never go all the way, even when that rotten judge sentenced him. But he was wrong. They hung him just the way they'll hang my pa," Bess said, and Fargo's brows lifted in question. "Pa won't give in, either. He won't clear out. He's told me so. They can hang him, but I'll still have the land, he said."

"Till they come after you," Fargo said.

"That's what I've tried to tell him, but Pa's a stubborn man. We have to stand up to them, no matter what. He's always believed in principles. They're saying he did it all on his own. They'll sentence him and hang him for it."

"No, they won't," Fargo said.

Bess Hanford's hand came out—a quick, impulsive gesture—touched his arm, and pulled away at once. "I thank you for trying to make me feel better, but there's no use," she said as she finished her drink.

"I saw the barn go up in flames and I saw four men ride away from it," Fargo said, and watched her eyes widen.

"You saw it?" she gasped.

"And I'll tell the judge what I saw," Fargo said. She flung herself against him, her arms curling around his neck and he felt the soft pressure of her breasts, the warm sweetness of her around him before she pulled back quickly. He saw the hope fade from her face even as he watched.

"I owe you again, for wanting to help," she said. "But it won't work. They'll hang him."

"No judge can ignore an eyewitness," Fargo said.

"They'll find a way," Bess said glumly.

"They can't," Fargo told her. "Now you just stop being so damn sure things will go wrong."

Her smile was sudden and sad, full of wry wisdom. "Thanks for being so sure things will go right," she said.

She leaned forward, brushed his lips with hers, pulled away quickly.

"You offering me passion or pork chops?" He grinned.

Her light-brown eyes grew thoughtful. "Pork chops. For now," she said.

"That'll do," he told her. "For now."

She rose and he watched her retreat into the kitchen, plump, rounded rear bouncing deliciously. Bess Hanford's pert prettiness, her open, frank honesty, set her apart from most women, he decided. No guile, no coyness to her, but a directness that was its own kind of sensuousness.

"Help yourself to another drink," she called from the kitchen, and he took the offer and sat back to enjoy the warmth of the whiskey as it curled itself inside him. When Bess called again, it was for supper. She served a hearty meal on a pine table at one side of the kitchen—thick pork chops, corn bread, and collard greens. When they finished, she turned the lamp on in the main room and folded herself on the worn green sofa next to him to sip on another glass of whiskey. The top buttons on her shirt had come open and he enjoyed the smooth, round curve of one high breast as she sat back.

"The pork chops were damn good," Fargo said. "I'm wondering if the passion's goin' to match."

Her light-brown eyes met the laughter in his glance with quiet seriousness. "You'll not be finding out tonight," she said. "I'm not for saying thanks that way. You ought to be hungry, not grateful, when you go to a man, I've always felt."

"Couldn't agree more," Fargo said. "You saying you're not hungry?"

She remained quietly thoughtful. "I'm saying I'm not ready. There's a difference," she answered.

"There is," he agreed. "I'm in no special hurry. I think you'd be worth waiting for, Bess Hanford."

"Compliments on top of rescuin'?" she said. "You go around the country doing just that?"

"Not usually." He laughed. "They call me the Trailsman."

Her light-brown eyes stayed on him, a long, studying stare. "I'm thinking you read people as well as trails," Bess said.

"One goes with the other," he told her.

"Anyway, I'm beholden to you for helping me today and for trying to help Pa tomorrow," Bess Hanford said, her pert face staying sober as she rose to her feet. "We've an extra room with a good cot in it. It's yours for the night," she said.

"Good enough," he said, and got to his feet as she lit a hurricane lamp and led the way to the room. It had a single window half-open, a washstand and big white porcelain pitcher, a cot, and a three-legged puncheon table beside it.

"Sleep well, Fargo," she said.

"You, too," he said, and watched her pull the door closed after her as she left. He undressed to his shorts and turned off the little lamp. The cot was six inches too short for him, but it was firmly comfortable and he relaxed and let thoughts drift idly through his mind. There were questions he hadn't asked of Bess, questions he wasn't sure he wanted to pursue. Taking her pa out of a hangman's noose was one thing. Getting involved in a land feud was something else. He'd be content to settle for the first, he mused silently, and maybe wait to see if Bess Hanford could get herself hungry enough or ready enough. He closed his eyes and let sleep come with the warm wind that sifted in through the half-open window.

He'd been asleep for at least three hours, he guessed,

when his mountain cat's hearing woke him, the sound hardly more than a soft murmur. But the sound was the unmistakable rattle of a rein chain, and the whinny of a horse drifted into the little room. Fargo was on his feet at once, pulling on trousers and gun belt. One long stride took him to the window, where, peering out into the night, he saw Bess emerging from the stable, pulling the brown mare behind her. He had on boots and was out of the house as she began to swing into the saddle. "Where in hell are you going?" he growled as he took hold of the mare's headstall.

Bess frowned, first in surprise, then in determination. "To get my pa out of jail," she said.

"You mean to get yourself shot," Fargo said.

"No, I'll get him out. I'll find a way," she insisted.

"Dammit, I told you I'd tell them what I saw, come morning." Fargo frowned back.

"And I told you they'll get around that," she said.

"They want to make everything look lawful. They can't do that and ignore an eyewitness," he told her.

"You don't know them," she said. "I'm getting him out of there tonight."

"Hell you are. I didn't save your hide from being bullwhipped so's you could get it shot full of holes," Fargo flung at her. "And that's sure as hell what'll happen if you go charging into that jail." She didn't answer, but the stubborn anger stayed in her eyes. "You getting off that horse or do I take you off?" he said.

Her answer was a quick pull on the reins that yanked the mare's head around and tore her away from his grip on the headstall. She slapped the mare on the rump and the horse started to leap forward, but Fargo dived, one arm swinging out to encircle the girl's waist. He yanked and she flew from the saddle as the mare went forward. He caught her in his arms as she struggled and tried to punch him.

"Dammit, you let me go," she hissed.

"When you stop being a little fool," he told her as he lifted her and carried her into the house. He saw the bedroom door open, entered the room, and tossed her onto the bed, where she bounced once and came to a stop. He saw tears held back in her eyes as she glared at him.

"You don't know them. They won't listen to you," she shouted.

"They'll have to," he said. "You breaking your pa out of jail will only make it look worse for him, even if you got lucky and pulled it off."

She rocked back and forth on her knees, her eyes closed. "You don't know them, you just don't know them," she chanted.

"Do I have to tie you up for the rest of the night?" he said, and she snapped her eyes open to peer at him.

"You wouldn't do that," she muttered. "Yes, you would," she corrected herself. "No, you don't have to do that," she said.

"I've your word you won't pull any more stunts like that one?" he pressed. She didn't answer and he kicked the door shut with his knee. "All right, there's not too much of the night left. I'll just bed down here. You make one move and I'll hear it," he said. He moved to the edge of the big double bed that took up most of the room, and pale moonlight affording just enough light to see, he pulled off gun belt and trousers and lay down on the bed in his shorts. Hands behind his head, he stretched and felt his powerful muscles ripple down his hard-packed frame. Bess hadn't moved as she watched him. "You won't be getting much sleep sitting on your knees that way," he said casually.

"I won't be sleeping any," she snapped, but she pulled herself up, swung her body around, and lay down on the other side of the bed.

"Suit yourself," he said, and he closed his eyes to tiny slits that let him barely see her as she lay on her back, high, very round breasts pushing almost straight upward. He lay that way, feigning sleep, and saw her turn her head to peer curiously at him. He watched as her eyes traveled up and down his body until finally she turned her back to him and settled herself on the pillow. He let sleep come to him, then. He snapped awake three times during the remainder of the night, but she was only turning fitfully on her side of the big bed. When morning came, he woke to look across at her. Sleep had refused denial and she lay with her eyes closed, her lips slightly parted, pert little face slightly stubborn even in sleep. He rose, pulled on trousers, gun belt, and boots, and silently went into the extra room to finish. Finally washed and dressed, he woke her gently.

She turned and sat up, startled, the middle button of her shirt popping open to let him glimpse the very round, tanned smoothness of one breast. She pulled the blouse closed at once, her frown instant as she pushed herself from the bed.

"I'll be out in a minute," she muttered crossly.

"I'll saddle up," he said. He left for the stable and had just finished saddling the Ovaro when she appeared, her eyes wide as she looked at him.

"You were wrong last night," she muttered. "You shouldn't have stopped me. You meant well, I know that, but you were wrong."

"You were wrong," he said sharply. "Now let's get to town. I want to speak my piece and get this done with."

Fargo's half-closed eyes snapped open, ending his drifting thoughts as the door slammed and he saw Judge Samuel Tolliver striding to his chair behind the makeshift bench. Black frock coattails trailing behind his long, spindly figure, he looked not unlike a tattered crow, Fargo reflected.

The judge banged his gavel on the bench. "Court's in session," he proclaimed. "It's time to decide this here case."

2

Fargo saw Judge Samuel Tolliver cast a quick, watery-eyed glance at him, his mouth pull together in the hint of a smug smile. "Sheriff, bring in those three new witnesses," the judge called out.

Fargo felt his eyes narrow as apprehension stabbed at him instantly, chilling, prodding. He half-turned in his seat to see the sheriff shepherding three men into the courtroom. The apprehension stabbed deeper as he watched the three men move toward the judge with shuffling steps. The first one had a face of alcohol-sodden cheeks, that particular kind of veined flush that lay over a barroom pallor. The second one had the dulled eyes of a borderline idiot, and the third man's hair and shirt were still wet from where he'd obviously been dipped into a pail of water to sober him up.

Fargo cursed silently as the apprehension turned into a block of ice in the pit of his stomach. He glanced at Bess and saw her sitting ramrod-straight in her chair, her round, pert face drawn tight.

"You three men step up here," Fargo heard the judge call out, and he turned his attention to the charade that had started to unfold in front of him. "You swear to tell the truth and nothing else?" the judge barked, and the three men mumbled their answers. "What's your name?" the judge asked the first, red-faced one.

"Lem Tenman," the man said.

"You see that barn burn down night before last?" Judge Tolliver asked, and the man nodded. "What else did you see?" the judge asked, his long face a gaunt mask.

"Saw Tom Hanford run away from it. Had a torch in his hand," the man muttered, never lifting his eyes to look up at the judge.

"All right, Lem. Step back," the judge said, and focused on the one with his mouth still hanging open. "What's your name?" he saked.

"Eb," the man said.

"Eb what?" Judge Tolliver said impatiently.

"Eb Cinder," the man said.

"You see the fire, too, Eb?" the judge asked, and the man nodded. "What else did you see, Eb?" the judge prodded.

Eb lifted his head, half-turned to where Bess's pa sat beside a deputy. He squinted, frowned, seemed to search the courtroom. "Saw that man run from the fire," he said finally.

"What man?" the judge pressed, and Eb frowned again. "Have the defendant stand up," the judge said, and the deputy pulled Tom Hanford to his feet. "That the man?" the judge asked, and Eb nodded.

Fargo felt the ice in the pit of his stomach turning to cold rage, and he realized his knuckles had turned white where his hand gripped the edge of his chair. Judge Tolliver turned his watery-blue eyes on the third man, the one with the still-wet hair and water-soaked shirt. "What's your name?" he asked.

"Zeke Ashford," the man said. "I saw the fire, too," he volunteered quickly.

Judge Tolliver nodded. "What else did you see?" he asked solemnly.

"Saw Tom Hanford run from it," Zeke Ashford said.

"You with Lem and Eb at the time?" the Judge questioned.

"No, your Honor, Judge, I was ridin' by alone," the man answered.

"All right, you've come forward. You're dismissed now," the judge said. The three men stayed motionless in front of him. "That means you can go now," he said, leaning forward, and Fargo watched the trio all but fall over each other in their haste to get to the door. Fargo saw Judge Tolliver's eyes turn to him as he rose to his feet. "You've said your piece, mister." the judge frowned.

"I've something else to say," Fargo said. "Those three bums were dragged in here to lie. This whole trial's a crock of shit."

The judge let his eyes grow horror-stricken. A good piece of acting, Fargo conceded. "How dare you say that about my courtroom?" the judge roared. "I'm holding you in contempt of court."

"You got the right word," Fargo bit out.

"You sit down. I'll deal with you later," the judge said.

"You sure will," Fargo said as he remained on his feet.

Judge Tolliver banged his gavel, turned his eyes on the spectators and back to the big man still standing. Fargo caught the flicker of crafty smugness that passed through the long face. "Three against one, Mister Fargo," the judge said. "I guess you saw wrong. Or maybe you're doing the lying. Maybe you're trying to protect the defendant." He banged the gavel again and turned to Sheriff Curry. "Have the defendant stand while I do the sentencing," he said. "Burning a barn and killing horses is the same as horse-stealing, far as I'm concerned. I hereby sentence Tom Hanford to be hung by the neck tomorrow morning. Case closed."

Fargo's eyes were blue quartz as they bored into the man, but Judge Tolliver kept his face turned away as he hurried from the room. Fargo looked to find Bess and was just in time to see her disappear out the door. He twisted his way through the crowd and reached the street. She was racing away on the brown mare, halfway to the end of town already, he saw, and he cursed under his breath. He paused as Sheriff Curry and two of his deputies took Bess's pa from the courtroom. The man seemed even smaller, more round-shouldered in their hands as they led him away. But his eyes were clear and his jaw tight, Fargo saw. He also noted that they put him in the town jail only a few doors from the courtroom.

He spun and pulled himself onto the Ovaro and sent the horse galloping from town and he cursed into the wind as he rode from Owl Creek. He had underestimated the extent of their scroungy cleverness. His testimony had blown their little charade apart. They had to do something to counter what he'd said, and they did it—crude and bald-faced, impossible to pull off with an honest judge—but it let them keep up their pretense of lawfulness. Three witnesses against one, all spoken out in open court. The pretense was important, he reflected, the outward appearance of lawfulness necessary for their game, whatever it was.

He pushed aside speculation and concentrated on sending the Ovaro up a shortcut, a steep slope that saved him minutes of riding, and he raced down the other side along a narrow pine trail. When he reached the valley, he turned the horse north and came to the house with the hog pens to one side just as Bess emerged, a big .44 Henry in her hands. She raised the rifle at once as she saw him skid to a halt, tears still staining her round cheeks.

"You stay right there, Skye Fargo. Don't you come near me," she warned.

He slowly climbed from the saddle and she raised the rifle further as she edged toward the brown mare. "What do you figure to do with that?" he asked.

"Don't you try to stop me again. I don't want to have to use this on you," Bess said.

"Put that down," he growled.

"No," she snapped. "I don't know that maybe you're not in it with them."

"You take leave of all your senses, girl?" He frowned.

"You stopped me from getting him out last night. They're very clever. Maybe they sent you to do that," she said.

"I'm going to forget you said that because you're too upset to think straight. Otherwise, I'd fan your little ass for that kind of damn-fool talk," Fargo returned.

"Anyway, you're not stopping me now. Maybe I won't get him out, but I'm going to get me a rotten, lying judge," Bess said.

"And get yourself hung by a real judge, if you're alive for it," Fargo said.

"I don't care. I'm going to try and you're not stopping me this time," Bess insisted.

"Didn't come to stop you. Came to help you," Fargo said.

"Well, you won't . . ." she began, and caught her words in midair. "You what?" She frowned.

"I came to help you. You said they'd find a way. I should've listened to you. I stopped you, instead. My mistake. I'll make it right now. I'll get your pa out," he said.

He saw the wariness in her eyes. "You mean that?" she asked.

"I say something, I mean it," Fargo growled. "You won't do it rushing in like a bull in a china shop." He walked toward her and saw the wariness pushed aside by hope as her eyes suddenly filled. She lowered the barrel of the big old Henry and he took it from her as she leaned against his chest, little half-sobs coursing through her.

"The bastards, the stinkin' bastards," she muttered as he felt the softness of her breasts against him, and she pulled back, eyes suddenly dry and wide with fear. "It'll be harder now. They'll have him under heavier guard. I know Roy Curry. He won't take chances," she said.

"Fix us some lunch while I do some thinking," he told her, and she nodded, brushed her face over her sleeve as she turned and strode into the house. It would give her something to do besides thinking about her pa, Fargo murmured to himself as he sat down on the doorstep. He leaned back against the door frame, watched a sow nursing a litter of eight piglets as he let his thoughts start to sort themselves into order. Barging in was sure to fail. It would bring on a shoot-out and more of the sheriff's deputies running to help.

Fargo's eyes narrowed as thoughts drifted slowly through his mind. The idea of an exchange held him for a moment, the judge for Tom Hanford. The judge was important, a major part of their little courtroom charade. But then maybe they'd be willing to sacrifice the judge. Perhaps he'd outlived his usefulness. Fargo let the idea slide away. There were too many uncertainties in it. He didn't even know who or what he was dealing with. All he knew was Bess's accusations about a man named Lansing and that he'd been party to a trial plainly set up to frame the defendant. It wasn't enough for bargaining hostages.

He drew a deep sigh. Tom Hanford had to be set free the hard way. That meant they had to get in and out fast, perfect timing in a plan that had a chance to succeed. He half-closed his eyes as he let his thoughts turn to the mechanics of planning an escape. He had discarded half a dozen ideas when Bess broke into his thoughts with a plate of bacon and eggs and sat down beside him with one for herself. "You come up with anything?" she asked between bites.

"Not yet. But I will," he told her. He ate quickly, more hungry than he'd realized, and when he finished, he saw Beth leaning back on her elbows, the smooth, high breasts pushing hard against the shirt as she studied him.

"You ever think maybe there's a reason things happen the way they do?" she asked. "Like your being there to help me and being here now?"

"You mean luck?" he said.

"No, luck's pure chance. I mean fate, a reason for things to be," she said.

"Most times, you make your own luck. Maybe you make your own fate, too," Fargo said.

"No, there's something more, I think, a reason why you've come along now. Some things are meant to happen," she said.

"I hope so." Fargo smiled, and she saw his eyes take in the firm, full roundness of her and she tossed him a disapproving glance.

"You've a one-track mind," she admonished.

"Damn nice track, though," he said, and she rose and took the plates into the house.

"Maybe I ought to just try to smuggle a gun in to Pa," Bess called out. "I'm allowed a last visit."

"You think they won't search you?" he called after her as he leaned back against the door frame and began to search for a plan again. But her words hung in the air and he found himself turning them in his mind. No smuggled gun. They'd be watching for that, he grunted. But they'd be watching her as she visited with her pa, watching and listening, and Fargo's brows knitted as the idea caught at him with gathering strength. It might be just enough, all their attention on her. All he needed was one quick moment, enough to take care of the guard without noise. No shooting, that was the key to it. Shots would bring others on the run. His lips pursed as plans began to take shape. He glanced up as Bess returned to stand over him in the doorway. "No gun, but you'll be paying your pa a visit," he said.

"You figure the guard will be busy watching me," she said, and he nodded.

"Hard enough for me to take him quick and quiet," he said, and paused to study her. "You know, this could all go wrong, real wrong," he said.

Her pert face nodded gravely. "I know that. I don't have my head in the clouds," she said with reprimand in her voice.

"So long as you know," he remarked.

"I've been thinking about that," Bess said. "How long will we be waiting here?"

"We've a while, till dark and the town quiets down. I want the streets pretty near empty," he said.

She turned to stand before him as he looked up at her. With one, quick motion, she pulled the buttons of her shirt open and he felt his frown melt with surprise and delight. "In case it goes wrong or in case it goes right," she said.

"I understand the first one but not the second," he said.

"I'll tell you after," she said, and she turned and strode into the house. The shirt flew open further, enough for him to glimpse the curved side of one high, full breast.

He rose and hurried inside after her, pulling off clothes as he followed her into her room. She was naked when he closed the door, one leg curled under her at the edge of the bed. Her body echoed her face, a pert little shape, all rounded curves, a short waist, legs that were shapely enough, a body a little chunky but bursting with vitality, a round little belly, and beneath it, an equally round little pubic mound with a dark, curly nap. She swung around to face him as he shed the last of his clothes and he saw the round, high breasts with firm and smooth, tiny pink tips set inside small, pink areolae.

He saw her eyes flick down to him as he stepped to her and he heard the short gasp that came from her. She reached arms up to encircle his neck and he pressed himself over her solid little body, his throbbing, pulsing organ resting against her round little belly.

"Jesus," she breathed. "Oh, God." He pressed his mouth over her sweet-soft lips, which answered him at once, and he felt the tip of her tongue sliding into his mouth, drawing back, thrusting forward again. She moved, pulled her lips back, and pushed one high, firm, full breast up at him, and he pulled it into his mouth, caressed the tiny pink nipple with his tongue.

"Oh, Oh, Jesus . . . oh, yes," she breathed, and he let his tongue move in a circle around the little tip. It rose, but hardly enough to push over the pink circle that surrounded it. He kissed, pulled, caressed each firm, high breast, and Bess uttered a soft little moaning sound. He felt her hands digging into the back of his neck, and he found her thighs with one hand, pushed between their young, firm flesh, stroked, and pressed, and her legs moved, stirred, drew up protectively, and then fell open. His hand moved down the inside of one young, firm thigh. He heard Bess gasp at its slow, unhurried progress.

His mouth pulled on one young breast as his hand touched the entrance to the moist portal, a tender touch that grew more demanding, and Bess cried out in her wanting as he caressed, slow, gentle motions. "Oh, oh, oh . . . oh, Jesus . . . oh, oh, oh . . . oh please, Fargo, please," she gasped as he buried his face into the little convexity of her belly, nibbled at her with the edge of his teeth. Her thighs drew up again and fell open, and he saw her torso half-twist, first one way then the other, and he drew his eager organ to her, pushed into the flowing warmth of her, and Bess Hanford screamed, a cry of shuddering ecstasy. "Aaaaaiiiiiii ... ah, ah, ah ... ah, good, good, oh, Jesus ... aaaaah," she breathed, gasped, cried out, words of pleading, and he moved deeper into her, felt the sweet sucking grasp of her around him.

Bess began to pump, her firm thighs rising to clasp around him, and suddenly her slightly chunky body had become a wildly pumping, thrusting, leaping package of ecstatic energy. "Come on, Fargo, come on ... more, more, yes, yes, yes," she murmured, pushing at him with her every pumping thrust. She was almost clinging to him in the air, her round, full rear hardly touching the bed as she held legs and arms around him and pushed and pumped, pulled and thrust, and he stayed with her as her cries began to rise, each one a notch higher, each little sound ascending a scale of pleasure. She never paused, her wild thrusting pumping never slowed. Suddenly her scream rose into the air and he felt her thighs tighten, her hands dig into his back. "Oh, God, Ah, ah, ah, God ... aaaaaaahhh ... oh, damn," Bess moaned inside the scream until suddenly the wild pushing of her pelvis halted and he felt the wetness of her curly black nap as she held against him. Her arms unlocked from around his neck and she fell back onto the bed as her thighs still stayed around him, and he watched the high, firm, full little breasts rise and fall as she drew in deep breaths. But the tiny pink nipples still stayed hard above the pink circles surrounding them, he noted, and he leaned forward, caressed each little tip with his tongue, and she moaned softly.

Her thighs grew soft finally, her legs sliding down his waist, and he drew from her to lay half atop her. Her eyes, half-closed, opened to stare at him. "I surprise you?" she asked.

"Nothing much surprises me, honey," he told her. "But I still want to know why in case it goes right."

Her lips formed a little smile. "You might be wondering if I was just being grateful, and I didn't want that," she said.

"Fair enough," he agreed, and cast a glance at the window, where the afternoon shadows were beginning to gather. "In case it goes right and in case it goes wrong. Seems to me you're owed one more."

Her little smile filled with anticipation. "Seems that way to me, too," she murmured, and pushed herself up over him, brought one high, firm breast down onto his lips. The tiny pink nipple was never going to come up any higher, he decided as he caressed it with his tongue, pulled gently on it, and felt it stay the same. He pulled in harder, drew most of her breast into his mouth and she gasped. "Ah, ah . . . ah, yes, good, oh, God," she murmured. When he let her slide from his lips, she drew back a moment, let her eyes move up and down his body, followed with her hand. "Oh, Jesus," she said as she closed her fingers around him. "Oh, Jesus."

"You been away from the well a long while," he ventured, and she nodded as she gripped him firmly.

"Owl Creek doesn't attract the kind of man I'd want to lie with," she said. "Until now."

"Luck," he said.

"Fate," she corrected soberly, and began to stroke his pulsing organ. "Jesus, take me quick, Fargo," she said suddenly, and her round little rear was lifting, her hips pumping into the air before he could swing over her. She thrust herself onto him as he moved forward, soft walls tightening around him. Once again, when her climax erupted, there was no slowing, no pause in her wild pumping, and only the gasped scream gave evidence of her coming and, of course, the warm wetness of her little nap as it pressed hard against him. As she had the first time, her arms fell away while her thighs stayed locked around him as she fell back onto the bed. Finally, her legs slid down as she uttered a long sigh and he came to lie beside her. The night had come, and he gently stroked her smooth, young skin.

"We've got to do some talking about tonight," he said, and she nodded, her pert face growing grave at once. She pushed up on one elbow, and the high, round breasts hardly dipped at all. "You might have to put your shirt on so's I can concentrate," he said.

"Try hard." She smiled, enjoying her own powers.

"You know what you're going to do," he began, and she nodded.

"Visit my pa as though it was a last visit for real," she said.

"No word to him, not even with your eyes, nothing that might make him frown, wonder, nothing that they might catch on to," Fargo said. "Nothing, understand?"

"I understand," she said. "I've an extra horse we can bring for Pa."

"Good," Fargo said, and swung from the bed. She leaned her face into his abdomen as she sat up, her arms encircling his waist. "Scared?" he asked.

"A little, I guess," she said. "For Pa, not for myself. He's a hung man if we don't get him out."

"Get dressed and stop thinking," he said gruffly and stepped back from her. He turned away and began to pull on clothes. He finished first and went out into the night. It was dark, a new moon that shed little light, and he grunted in satisfaction. Every little bit helped. When Bess emerged, she was dressed in a black skirt and dark-green scoop-necked blouse that let the swell of her breasts rise in delicious loveliness. She saddled the extra horse and he was waiting on the Ovaro when she finished. She rode in silence beside him as he moved across the valley and headed toward Owl Creek. He finally halted when he reached the edge of town. "You wait here," he said. "Give me five minutes, then go on to the jail.

She nodded, her pert little face sober, and he took the reins of the extra horse and led the animal behind him as he circled back of the houses that lined Main Street. He rode almost to the back of the jailhouse before dismounting. There was no back door to the jail, he noted. There'd be only the front door out. He hitched the Ovaro and the extra horse under a low-branched chestnut and went forward on foot, along the side of the jailhouse. He halted when he reached the front corner that faced the street and saw two deputies outside the door of the jail. He recognized both. The one with the buckskin jacket still had a bandage across the top of his hand. The other was the thin, spidery-legged man. He expected there'd be two. One would go inside with Bess, the other most likely stand guard outside. He dropped to one knee as he saw Bess ride up at a fast trot and swing from the brown mare.

The man in the buckskin jacket threw her a leering grin instantly. "Well, look what we've got here, the everlovin' daughter," he said.

"I've come to see my pa. I've a right," Bess snapped.

"Sure you do, honey. Sheriff said to let you in if you showed. We do things decent around here," the man sneered. "Where's that big friend of yours that's lookin' for a gut full of lead?"

"He left," she said. "I want to go in."

The man turned to the spidery-legged deputy. "You stay out here. I'll take the little lady inside," he ordered as he opened the door and followed Bess inside the jail. The other man shifted, leaned against a post beside the door of the jail. Fargo's eyes squinted along the dark street. It was empty. He rose, pulled his hat down, and hunched his shoulders forward as he moved into the open. The spidery-legged figure outside the door straightened up at once, hand on his gun as he watched the figure lurch alongside the building. Fargo half-crashed against the wall, hung there for a moment, then lurched forward again, head bent down, his body rubbery.

"You, get out of here," the man shouted. Fargo seemed to pause on uncertain legs, and then he stumbled forward, lurched sideways at the guard. The man grabbed at him. "Damn drunk, get out of here," he snarled, and Fargo felt the man's hand close around his collar. Fargo's short, right blow drove upward with the force of all his shoulder muscles. The man doubled in two like a jackknife, and Fargo brought the butt of his Colt down on the back of his neck. He caught the doubled-over man with one hand and eased him silently to the ground. Pulling the inert figure away from the doorway, he edged alongside the window and peered in. He cursed silently as he saw another guard inside the room.

The one with the buckskin jacket had Bess against the wall. "Now, I can't let you go in to see your pa without searching you, can I?" He grinned. "That wouldn't be doing my job." Fargo saw Bess stay rigid, her face made of helpless fury as the man reached both hands down the neck of her blouse. "Not hiding any gun down there, are you, sweetie?" He grinned. "Jesus, those are a nice pair." The man laughed as Bess stayed with her eyes closed, her jaw fixed, and Fargo saw him bring his hands out from inside the blouse to begin to run them up her skirt.

"Hey, don't I get to search her some?" Fargo heard the second guard ask, a stocky man with a pitted face.

"You can search her when she comes out, Sam," the spidery-legged one said. He laughed, and Fargo saw his hands moving under the skirt, come around to fasten onto Bess's round little rear.

"Bastard," Bess yelled, her eyes snapping open. She swung and he half-ducked, half-fell away to avoid the blow.

"Open the cell door, Sam," he said, laughing. "Let her go in and see her pa."

The other one opened the cell door and Fargo saw Bess go inside. The cell was in half-darkness. He could only see the shadowy shapes of Bess and her pa as they embraced. He returned his attention to the two guards and swore silently again. He'd figured on only one inside, but the extra one proved an unexpected obstacle. There was no way to take them silently one at a time, not unless both had their attention riveted on something. He shot a glance up the dark street. It was still empty, but he had the uneasy feeling he was treading on the edge of his luck.

Inside the jail the two guards had their backs to him, but they were a few feet apart and he strained his ears to hear their suddenly low-voiced exchange. "Why not?" he heard the spidery-legged one say. "Soon as you let her out and lock the cell."

"In front of her pa?" Fargo heard the other one ask.

"Hell, he ain't gonna be around to tell." The other one laughed.

The slow smile that spread over the pitted face was one of anticipation. Fargo felt the stab of irony as he realized they were going to give him that moment of complete preoccupation he needed. His eyes probed into the dimness of the cell. Bess was prolonging the visit, no doubt wondering what was holding him back. She was trying to help, but doing just what he didn't want her to do now. Of course, she'd no way of knowing that and he swore under his breath again as he cast another glance down the street. It was still empty but his uneasiness grew. He returned his eyes to the window and saw the spidery-legged guard move toward the cell, the other man following. Fargo muttered a silent thanks to the impatience of lust.

"Enough, girlie," he heard the spidery-legged one call out. "Visit's over."

"No, I want more time," Fargo heard Bess say, panic in her voice.

"No more time. You coming out or do we drag you out?" the man said harshly, and Fargo watched as Bess turned to her pa, hugged him in a last embrace, and backed from the cell. He saw her move into the lighted part of the jail, her face drawn with uncertainty, her eyes moving around the room.

"Now you can visit with us, honey," Fargo heard the one called Sam say.

Bess turned, read his face at once, and tried to bolt for the door. Both men seized her, dragged her back, and one grabbed her legs, yanked, and she landed on the floor. The spidery-legged one held her arms pulled over her head as Sam pushed her skirt up and started to kneel down over her.

"Leave her, goddamn you, leave her," Fargo heard her pa shouting.

"Jesus, look at that little beaver," Sam chortled as he ripped at Bess's clothes.

Fargo moved to the door, closed his hand around the knob, and turned slowly, carefully, the tiny click of the door opening drowned in the men's leering laughter. He stepped silently into the room. Both men were intent on Bess as she tried helplessly to twist away from them. Sam pulled his trousers open and started to press himself down over the girl's pelvis, forcing her legs apart. She cried out in pain.

Fargo, the big Colt in his hand, moved with the quickness of a cougar's strike, his hand bringing the barrel of the gun around in a sideways sweep. The barrel smashed into the spidery-legged one's face splitting his forehead open, and smashing his nose into a bloody mess. Fargo didn't wait to see the man's eyes cross and glaze as his body fell back in an inert heap. Fargo brought the gun barrel up in a tremendous uppercut as Sam looked up, his eyes widening in surprise. The gun smashed into his jaw and Fargo heard the snapping sound of the jawbone as it broke in two. The man's face seemed to collapse, his jaw a loose, flapping appendage as blood bubbled from his mouth. Fargo's kick smashed in the side of his cheekbone and sent him sprawling halfway across the jailhouse floor.

Bess pushed herself to her feet as Fargo stepped to the still, silent figure and pulled the cell keys from the man's pocket. He tossed them to Bess. "Get your pa out," he said as he went to the door, opened it a fraction, and peered out. His lips drew back in a grimace. "Goddamn," he hissed as he saw Sheriff Roy Curry and two of his men walking toward the jail. Bess appeared at his shoulder, her pa beside her, a small man, stoop-shouldered, his quick eyes still alert as they glanced at the big man.

"His name's Fargo, Pa," Bess said. "I'll explain later."

"Trouble," Fargo bit out, and Bess peered under his arm to see through the opening.

"Roy Curry," she gasped.

"You run for it. I'll cover you. The extra horse is under a chestnut back of the jail," Fargo said. He turned, blew the lamp out, and kicked the door open. He saw the sheriff halt at once as he saw the light go out. Bess raced from the jail, her pa beside her, both vaulting onto her brown mare. Fargo fired three shots and saw Sheriff Curry and his two men dive for cover as Bess raced down the narrow passage between the two buildings. Fargo edged from the jail, stayed in the deepest shadows, and fired another three shots in the general direction of where the sheriff had dived for cover. He rose to a crouch, ran around the edge of the jail and down the passageway.

"Get inside. See what the hell's inside," he heard the sheriff yell. Two shots followed him as Fargo raced to the end of the passageway. He ducked right, then left, and reached the deep shadows under the chestnut. He paused to reload, fired a volley into the passageway, and heard the sound of footsteps scrambling backward. Vaulting onto the Ovaro, he sent the horse into a full gallop and streaked east away from Owl Creek. He slowed after a few minutes. The sheriff wouldn't be coming after anyone, not right away. But he'd come, as soon as he surveyed what had happened in his jail and rounded up a posse. Fargo turned the Ovaro north and headed for the valley.

He reached the slope into the lush green land as the new moon climbed high into the sky on its way to the horizon, and he rode west, slowing when he saw the light stabbing into the darkness. Bess and her pa came out of the house when he rode to a halt and dismounted. Tom Hanford stepped forward with his hand outstretched. "Bess told me about what you've done. I'm indebted to you, Fargo," the man said.

"Pa insisted on waiting to thank you himself. I wanted him to ride on," Bess put in.

"She's right. You'd best hightail. They'll come looking sooner or later," Fargo said.

"Stinkin' bastards," Bess cut in. "Pa said Judge Tolliver paid him a visit with his usual offer."

"That's right," Tom Hanford said, his quick eyes hardening. "I sign away all rights to my land and promise to clear out and he'd give me a pardon. I told him to go to hell." Tom Hanford straightened his stooped shoulders for a moment of angry pride. He reminded

Fargo of a terrier he'd once known, old and tired but with still enough terrier inside him to hang on when he had to.

"You get moving now, Pa. Ride to the campgrounds and stay there," Bess said.

"I can't stay there. I don't want to get the others in trouble. I'm an escaped prisoner," her pa said.

"You can stay there till morning," Bess insisted. "They won't go looking there till then."

"I suppose so," Tom muttered gravely as he pulled himself onto the horse. "Much obliged, Fargo. Bess said you'd be staying on to help out. That makes me feel better." With a quick wave, he sent the horse into a canter and the night swallowed him up in moments.

Fargo's eyes bored into Bess and he saw her face draw a veil over itself. "Anyone ever tell you not to lie to your pa?" Fargo growled.

"I told him that so's he wouldn't worry," she said as she turned to meet his stare.

Fargo's eyes stayed hard. "What's this campground you mentioned?" he asked.

"Most of the people who lost their lands have set up a camp at the other end of the valley," she said as she started into the house.

"Why?" Fargo asked, his question simple curiosity.

She half-shrugged and closed the door. "They keep hoping to find a way to get their land back," she said, and he saw her pause, a little note of craftiness creep into her eyes.

"Forget it," he snapped harshly.

"I didn't mean anything," she said.

"Hell, you didn't," he growled.

"All right, so I did," she said, dropping all pretense. She came to him, her arms circling his neck. "You could do it, Fargo. You could help them. They need someone to stop Dorrance Lansing, someone to help them fight back. Pa and I are a part of it now."

"You still have your land," Fargo said.

"Pa's an escaped prisoner. How long do you think they'll let me stay on?" Bess countered.

"Not long," he agreed.

"Don't you care?" She frowned, her pugnaciousness rising at once.

"I got your pa out of jail. I'm out of the good-deed business," he returned.

"You're just going to walk away?" she accused, stepped back to glare at him.

"Ride away," he corrected.

"I thought you cared more about what's right," she snapped.

"You thought wrong," he said.

Her lips tightened and she glared at him. "All right, you don't care enough about what's right or doing any more good deeds. You care about money, don't you?" she said.

He watched the hurt and anger that clouded her face. "It helps," he said mildly.

"Then we'll all get together on it and pay you," she said, making it sound like a reproof.

"To do what?" he asked.

"Stop Dorrance Lansing. Prove that he's been behind everything that's happened. Clear Pa's name and get everybody's land back," Bess shot at him.

"Maybe that just can't be done," he said.

"We've got to try," she insisted.

"You talk to the others about this?" he asked.

"No," she admitted.

"Maybe you'd better do that," he said, and she glared at the condescension in his voice.

"I will, come morning. They'll go along. I know they

will. There's been talk about finding somebody to help us," Bess said.

"And I'm right here and handy." Fargo smiled. "Fate, again?"

Her eyebrows lifted coolly. "Yes," she snapped.

"But fate nudged with hard cash," he said.

"It's still fate," she insisted, ignoring his smile. A sound from outside broke off the conversation. Hoofbeats, a half-dozen horses riding hard. He stepped back from the door and drew the big Colt on his hip.

"That'll be the good sheriff," Fargo said. "You do the honors."

Bess pulled the door open and Fargo peered out through the crack alongside the hinge. The sheriff and six of his men came to a halt as Bess stepped outside. Sheriff Roy Curry's small features seemed even more drawn together in the big, square head. "Where is he?" the sheriff rasped.

"Where's who?" Bess answered.

"You know damn well who. Your pa, you helped him escape," Sheriff Curry roared.

Fargo heard the pugnaciousness flare in Bess's voice at once. "Did you see me, Roy Curry?" she threw back. "Did you? No. You're all talk."

"Didn't have to see you. It was you and that Fargo feller," the sheriff said.

"You oughtn't to indulge in loose talk, Sheriff," Fargo said as he stepped from behind the door. The sheriff's eyes widened, then grew narrow as he took in the big man with the Colt in his hand.

"I got two deputies, one dead from gagging on his own blood, the other damn near dead with his face smashed to pieces. This little thing didn't do that by herself," Sheriff Curry growled.

"I don't think she did it at all," Fargo said.

"You're buckin' for real trouble, Fargo," the sheriff warned.

"Her pa's not here," Fargo said.

"You can go in and look for yourself," Bess added.

Sheriff Curry's small features stayed drawn in as he eyed Bess. "No need. You wouldn't be offering if he was there," he said as he pulled his horse around. "He's got too big a start now, but we'll find him tomorrow," he said to his men, and let his eyes fasten on the big man with the lake-blue eyes. "Meddling in other people's business can get you in trouble, Fargo," he rasped.

"So can dragging false witnesses into a courtroom," Fargo returned calmly. The sheriff kicked his horse into a fast trot and disappeared into the night with his men.

Bess strode into the house and closed the door after Fargo as he followed. Her eyes searched his face. "Any question we need help?" she speared.

"No question," he said. "Doesn't change anything, though."

"Of course not. That'd be asking too much," she said with icy sarcasm.

"I'll bed down outside," he said, and she took a moment to answer.

"No need for that," she snapped as she strode to her room. "Good night," she tossed back, and pulled the door shut.

He went into the extra room and undressed to shorts, a wry smile edging his lips as he stretched out on the cot. He let the warmth of the night move over his powerful body and had almost fallen asleep when he heard the door open. He lay still as she slid onto the cot beside him.

"This won't change anything, either," he remarked.

"Don't expect it to," she snapped.

He smiled in the dark. She lied, of course. Expectation was built in, as much a part of her as the wanting, even if she didn't admit it to herself. He turned as she reached for him, and her torso had already started to slide up and down along the cot. Response pushed aside reflections as he grew throbbingly hard for her. Enjoyment was its own reward. Bess echoed his thoughts with her body as she came over him, sought, found, cried out, her wanting almost desperate until, finally, her scream trailed away and he slept with her firm, chunky body hard against him.

3

He felt her wake early and he feigned sleep as she left the room with small, barefoot steps. He listened to her wash and dress and heard her hurry outside. She walked the horse from the stable until she'd gone a half-dozen yards from the house, then she swung onto the saddle and hurried away. Fargo lay on the cot for another hour of half-sleep, relaxed, and then he rose to go to the front door, where the morning sun bathed his nakedness. He washed and dressed leisurely, made himself coffee, and found two biscuits. After breakfasting, he sank down in the doorway to wait. But thoughts kept skipping through his mind, disjointed wanderings, all mixed together.

He'd come a long way on a wild-goose chase. Returning with pay in his pockets appealed to him. But he found himself hoping the others would turn down Bess Hanford's idea. He'd be playing against a loaded deck, a powerful man with the sheriff and the town judge on his payroll. And perhaps a scheme too far along to turn back now. Fargo let a small sigh hiss from his lips as he stretched. Maybe he could pick up something easy to do, a nice wagon train to take through, he mused. But his thoughts continued to slip over each other in slow disarray. The nights with Bess would be part of it, and that beckoned to him. He'd stayed other places for less, he reflected. There was a distinctly open, unvarnished, and pugnacious appeal to her lovemaking.

His thoughts were still idly drifting when a lone horseman rode into view and headed toward him. Fargo shifted position in the doorway so that his hand rested alongside the Colt as the man drew close enough for Fargo to see the deputy's badge glint in the sun. He stayed where he sat as the rider came to a halt. He was a man with cold gray eyes and a face covered by heavy stubble.

"Sheriff Curry sent me. He wants to see you in town at his office," the man said.

"He ordering or asking?" Fargo remarked mildly.

The man paused for a second. "Askin'," he answered.

Fargo nodded. "Tell him I'll stop by," he said.

"When?"

"When I get there," Fargo said.

The man turned his horse and rode away.

Fargo's lips pursed as the sheriff's messenger disappeared over the top of the rise. No casual invitation for tea, he grunted. Sheriff Curry probably hoped to smooth-talk him or scare him off. He'd fail either way. But it'd be interesting to hear him out, Fargo pondered, even if he decided against staying on. He pushed himself to his feet as the sun rose higher into the sky and went to the stable behind the house. He took the curry from his saddlebag and gave the Ovaro a good brushing, rubbed him down with a damp towel, and had just started to saddle the horse when Bess rode up. She had on a blue-and-white-checked shirt, he saw, and he read the satisfaction in her pert face.

"It's settled," she said. "Five hundred dollars. Everybody's putting in their share." He listened without comment and heard her voice bristle. "That's a good piece of money," she said.

"A fair piece of money," he corrected.

"It's all we could afford," she said as he pulled on the saddle strings. He finished tightening the cinch ring in silence. "Well, dammit?" she flung at him.

"You could be throwing your money away," he muttered.

"Why?"

"This could be past turning around," he said, meeting her eyes.

"Maybe," she conceded. "We have to try anyway."

"The sheriff has a passel of sidewinders. What if it comes down to a showdown?" Fargo said.

"We can match him," she said. "Now let's go. The others want to meet you, especially Charlie Burrows."

"Who's he?" Fargo questioned as he pulled himself into the saddle.

"Charlie's sort of held us all together. He's been a real leader. Charlie's got a lot of strength in him," Bess said as she turned her brown mare in a circle. Fargo nodded, glad there was at least one man among them he could count on. "Fastest way is down the middle of the valley," Bess said as he swung in beside her. She set a fast pace and he let his eyes sweep the valley on both sides as they rode. Lush land. Good, thick, green timber. Good land for farming, cattle, hogs, or just homesteading. But there was a lot of land just like it on both sides of the valley.

"Why?" he asked, and saw Bess frown. "Why this land?"

"Land's land if you're greedy," she answered.

Her answer had enough truth in it, yet it failed to satisfy. Something more, he sensed. His gaze swept the ridges again. This was Ute and Cheyenne land and sometimes the Arapaho drifted down from the north.

But the valley was quiet and he saw only an occasional Indian pony print as they rode. "Your pa there?" he asked Bess as they reached the end of the valley.

"No, he rode on this morning. He wouldn't stay and get the others in trouble for harboring an escaped convict," Bess said. "Roy Curry won't send his hounds too far after him. He has other things to do."

"Such as?"

"There are only three families left with land in the valley. He'd be moving against them unless you can stop him," she said. "Which means stopping Dorrance Lansing."

Fargo didn't reply as the land rose sharply and he rode over the crest of the rise to rein in as the collection of structures spread out in front of him. The tents caught his eye, first. No Indian tepee-style tents of buffalo and antelope hides, these were fashioned of white man's canvas and tarpaulin, higher and longer in shape. He counted six of the crude tents, and beyond he saw two big Conestoga wagons spaced apart with tarpaulin stretched across to form roof and sides of a square, boxlike structure. A wooden lean-to and an earthen hut with a thatched roof were the last dwellings.

"Pretty primitive stuff," Fargo observed.

"They set up here one by one, starting last spring," Bess told him. "Nobody figured what they'd do. They just leaned on each other. Now they need help."

Fargo reined to a halt as the figures emerged from the crude dwellings and tents. First to reach him was a small figure, not more than five-four, Fargo guessed, a shock of white hair on a lined face with a small beard almost as white as his hair. The little man looked at him with bright-blue eyes that were full of shrewdness. Eighty years of shrewdness, Fargo guessed.

"Charlie Burrows, Fargo," Bess said.

The little man's snapping blue eyes peered up at him

with a hint of laughter in them. "Don't look so disappointed," Charlie Burrows said.

"Let's say surprised," Fargo answered.

"Call a spade a spade. Disappointed," the little old man snapped, and Fargo's half-shrug was an admission. "Bess has a way of sweetening things when she wants something," Charlie said.

Fargo glanced at Bess. She avoided his eyes, stared at the others as they came up to form a semicircle. "Seems that way," he growled. A woman stepped forward, with a man beside her and two boys, about ten or twelve years old. The man, thin-faced and sad-eyed, nodded greetings. "Ned Simmons. This is my wife, Ruth," he said. "And my boys, Ned Junior and Biff."

Fargo nodded, read the man instantly as a good, plodding homesteader.

A little woman beside Ned Simmons peered at him from beneath gray-white hair drawn back tight on her head. In height and age she looked a perfect match for Charlie Burrows. "Abby Weeden," she announced, her voice clear and strong.

A stolid man with a wife and little blond girl moved forward next. "Fred and Nora Thompson," Bess introduced.

Fargo turned his eyes to the three young men that stepped forward, all with the same strong jaws, the same heavy brows, and curly dark hair. One, older than the others, perhaps thirty, Fargo guessed, spoke up quickly. "Ollie Joust," he said. "My brothers, Tad and Kelby. Heard about you, Fargo, when I lived in Minnesota. You can count on us for whatever you need to do."

"Good," Fargo said with as much enthusiasm as he could muster. He turned to the narrow-shouldered young man nearby and took in a nervously intense face, slightly hawklike, eyes that darted in quick glances and a mouth that turned down at one corner with a nervous twitch. The young woman at his side was a striking contrast, very subdued, eyes that seemed almost dull and certainly shy as they cast a quick glance back. Brown hair piled atop her head, she was not unattractive despite a held-in quality to her, hands clasped in front of her, her figure concealed in a very plain, straight gray dress.

"Ted Fuller and his sister, Mary," Bess said.

"You going to be able to do something for us, Fargo?" Ted Fuller blurted out almost demandingly.

"Maybe," Fargo answered. He glanced at the last figure to come forward, a woman with a little girl about six years old.

"Nell Owens," Bess said, and Fargo took in the woman's calm glance, her prematurely gray hair. She was pushing forty, he estimated but with a face that seemed ten years younger, with unlined skin, broad, flat cheekbones, a wide mouth, and a short, slightly heavy nose. A tall woman, Nell Owens had wide shoulders, ample hips, and heavy breasts under the plain dress she wore. In her eyes he saw tiredness, almost resignation, and a hint of curiosity as she met his glance. "Nell was the first one they railroaded," Bess said. "She was easy, a woman living alone with a little girl. She and Lansing had words about her letting some of her stock water at his water holes. They accused her of trying to poison his water a few days later."

Fargo's eyes had stayed on Nell Owens and saw the woman's broad face offer a wry smile. "Had two witnesses that saw me try to do it," she said with bitterness.

"I'll be back," Fargo said, his eyes sweeping over the others. "There'll be time for more talking." He wheeled the Ovaro, and Bess came alongside as he rode slowly away. He felt her eyes on the hard line of his jaw.

"Go on, say it," she snapped. "I know what you're thinking." His eyes turned on her and he speared her through half-lowered lids, letting the glance speak for itself. Her pugnaciousness refused instant retreat. "I told you they could stand up to Roy Curry's men in a showdown and you're thinking I knew better."

"Now, why would I think that?" Fargo asked innocently. "A pair of antiques, farmers, family men, women alone with kids, one feller so nervous his mouth twitches, and three men who could maybe hold their own."

She looked away and glowered. "Maybe you can avoid a shooting showdown," she muttered.

"I'd sure as hell try," he grunted.

"You want to back out?" she flared defensively.

"I'm thinking about it," he answered.

"No, you can't," Bess said, instant panic seizing her voice, and he saw her round eyes grow wide, blink at him. "We have no chance unless you help us. You can see that," she said.

He nodded agreement with her words. "That was all of them, I take it," he said.

"Except for Thea," Bess said.

"Thea?"

"Thea Manning. She'll be back, come nightfall. She went all the way to Saddle Rock with the wagon to pick up supplies," Bess said. "Does it every few weeks."

"Alone?" Fargo questioned, and Bess nodded. "Why not one of the men?" he asked.

"She volunteered. Seems the owner of the general store in Saddle Rock is an old family friend. He gives her a break in prices. Thea Manning's the kind who can take care of herself," Bess said.

He caught something in the last sentence and shot a quizzical glance at Bess. "Sounds like you're not real fond of Thea Manning," he suggested.

Bess shrugged, but her eyes, suddenly too bland, failed to match the careful words. "I've nothing against her," she said. "Fact is, she's very popular with most everybody. She's got a way of taking charge. She's just not my kind of person."

"Woman usually says that about a woman who's better-looking than she is," Fargo observed dryly, and drew an instant glare.

"Not in this case," Bess said sharply.

He smiled inwardly and tossed a question at her that had been jabbing at him. "You say the sheriff's railroaded them all on Dorrance Lansing's orders. Why has he let them band together there in a camp at the end of the valley?"

"He figures he has nothing to worry about. So far, he's been right. You saw how they're living, like gypsies. Nobody can stay the winter. They'll all have to run before the first snows come. They'll run to wherever they can. Me too. With everybody scattered, it'll all be over once and for all. You're our last chance, Fargo," she said.

He pursed his lips in thought for a moment. "You heading back to your place?" He frowned at her.

"Just to pick up some of my things. I don't think it's wise for me to stay on alone. Can't tell what Roy Curry or Judge Tolliver will think up to do," Bess said.

"I agree," he said. "I'll see you tonight when I get back," he said, halting his horse.

"I thought you were riding with me. Where are you going?" Bess asked quickly.

"To Owl Creek. The sheriff sent me an invitation to come talk with him," Fargo told her.

"You're not going, are you?" she asked in alarm. "He's setting a trap for you."

"The thought came to me, but I don't think so, not this time," Fargo answered.

"Then why'd he call you in to see him?" Bess insisted.

"Don't know. Maybe a fishing expedition, to find out if I'm going to move on. I'll let you know tonight," he said.

"I'll be staying with Abby Weeden till I set up my own tent," Bess said. She paused, frowned earnestly at him. "I wish you wouldn't go," she said.

"You worrying for me or for yourself and the others?" He grinned.

"Both, maybe," she threw back, and sent her horse into a canter.

He laughed and turned the Ovaro toward Owl Creek in a slow trot. It was late afternoon when he reached the town and he slowed, walked the horse down the wide street, passed the sheriff's office. Roy Curry sat behind a small desk inside, alone, and Fargo's eyes searched out the nearby doorways and the small spaces between buildings. Satisfied they concealed no waiting figures, he turned the Ovaro and rode back to the sheriff's office. He saw the man inside get to his feet as he dismounted and walked to the door.

"I'd about given up on your coming in today, Fargo," Roy Curry said. His big, block head sat on his shoulders as though it were a chunk of granite, the small features clustered together in the center continued to seem misplaced.

"Your man said you wanted to talk to me," Fargo remarked.

"Make yourself comfortable," the sheriff said, and gestured to a wooden chair with curved arms. Fargo's eyes flicked through the window to the street outside before he eased himself into the chair. The sheriff tried a smile that succeeded only in being unctuous. "Got a message for you and some advice," he said.

"I'm listening," Fargo said.

"Now, I know you helped out the Hanford girl, maybe even got yourself a piece of tail for it, and that's fine with me," the man began.

Fargo's voice was cold steel as he cut in. "You don't *know* anything of the kind, and I don't give a shit what's fine or isn't fine with you," he bit out. "You got anything more important to say?"

Fargo watched the sheriff control his temper with an obvious effort, keeping the smile on his lips. "Just trying to give you some advice, Fargo. Those valley people aren't worth bothering yourself about. I'd forget about 'em and go my way, if I were you. Nobody around here ever liked them."

"By nobody you mean Dorrance Lansing," Fargo said.

"No, I mean folks in general. They never came to town 'less they had to, never mingled with anybody, always kept to themselves. Little land grubbers, they were, small fry taking up good land. Judge Tolliver always said they were a shiftless, troublesome lot, and it's proved out he was right."

"I imagine Judge Tolliver often proves out his own words," Fargo said.

"Well, they're not worth getting your neck in a noose over, believe me," Sheriff Curry said, adopting an avuncular tone that did little to change the warning in his words.

"I take it that's the advice. What's the message?" Fargo said curtly.

"Dorrance Lansing wants to see you," the sheriff said, and Fargo felt his brows lift in surprise.

"He have some more advice for me?" Fargo asked.

"Can't say," the sheriff answered. He was still being careful, and Fargo decided to dig at him again.

"You always carry messages for Dorrance Lansing, sheriff?" he asked. "You run errands for him, too?"

The man's eyes hardened and the smile vanished. Fargo saw Roy Curry's knuckles grow white as his hands tightened on the arms of the wooden chair. But the man reined himself in. "From what happened, Mr. Lansing figured I might be talking to you," the sheriff said. "He got excited when he heard you were in town. Seems you've a reputation."

"Where's his spread?" Fargo asked.

"Start for the valley. Take the hill when you come to a double elm, head due north, and you'll see it," the sheriff said as Fargo rose to his feet. "Some folks have made a nice piece of change by cooperating with Dorrance Lansing," he added with studied casualness.

"I'll keep that in mind, coming from someone who ought to know," Fargo said.

The sheriff's mouth hardened and his eyes bored into the big man in front of him. "Fargo, I hope we won't be having anything more than friendly words," he said ominously.

"I'd hope for that, too, if I were you," Fargo said as he pulled the door open and stepped from the office. He paused to look back. "Give my regards to Judge Tolliver," he said. He climbed onto the Ovaro and rode slowly out of town toward the valley. He was surprised and curious as all hell, he admitted to himself. Dorrance Lansing's summons was not just more of the same, he was certain, not just another round of advice and thinly veiled warnings. That wouldn't make sense. It'd be too transparent. Lansing had to have two reasons for wanting to see him, the real one and the one he'd offer as a reason. Whatever it was, it was a bold approach and Fargo felt himself growing more intrigued as he rode.

He found the double elm, two trees twisted together, their separate trunks only inches apart. Just about to turn north, he saw the horse and rider racing toward him, the blue-and-white-checked shirt bright in the sunlight.

Bess skidded the mare to a halt, her face flushed. "Been looking for you. Come on, there's been trouble at John and Harriet Waller's place. Some of Roy Curry's men were there," she said, and wheeled the mare around. She raced off and left him to catch up to her. "It's not far, just below my place at the mouth of the valley," she said as he came up beside her. "Looks like Roy Curry's trying to pull off another of his lyin' swindles."

Fargo decided not to mention his impending visit with Dorrance Lansing as he raced beside her. They turned south when they reached the mouth of the valley. He saw the place the moment they dipped down, a house and barn and unfenced pasture land with maybe thirty steers on it. A small knot of figures was gathered at the front of the house, angry voices raised as he neared. He took in the bearded man in overalls, the woman beside him, and the boy and girl huddled together nearby.

"I told you I don't know how Lansing's steers got mixed in with my herd," Fargo heard the man say to the five figures on their horses. "Maybe they wandered down on their own or maybe they were brought down."

"You better watch your mouth, saying a thing like that," one of the deputies growled, a man with a bulbous nose and a torn gray shirt. He turned as Fargo rode up with Bess, and his eyes narrowed.

"What's the trouble?" Fargo asked, keeping his voice even.

"Cattle stealing, that's the trouble and we're takin' him in for it," the man said as he pointed to John Waller.

"Rubbish," Bess spit out.

"Get the hell out of here, both of you," the man snarled, and his bulbous nose reddened. "This is official business. We're here on the sheriff's orders."

Fargo looked past the man to John Waller. "Is it true? Are some of Lansing's cattle in with yours?" he asked.

"Yes, but I didn't steal them," Waller protested.

"Judge Tolliver will decide that," the big-nosed deputy cut in.

"*Hah!*" Bess snorted. "Do something," she hissed at Fargo.

Fargo moved the pinto back a pace, his voice a whisper loud enough for only her to hear. "Not now," he said. "I'd only be getting everyone in deeper. They'd like that. The law will all be on their side. Lansing's steers are in his herd. He'll have to go before Tolliver, first."

"You know what that'll mean," Bess returned.

"Maybe not this time. Maybe I can get to Lansing," he said and her glance was rejection.

Bess frowned over his words for a moment and then moved her mare forward. "Hold tight for now, John. We'll see you get a fair trial," she said. "Trust us. I'll stay with Harriet and the youngsters for a spell."

The woman smiled as gratefully as her fear would allow. The five men formed a semicircle around John Waller and he nodded in acceptance. The sheriff's crew looked at one another in smug self-satisfaction and rode off.

Fargo watched the man with the bulbous nose take the lead, and his eyes narrowed. He turned the Ovaro and cantered away, back toward the double elm, his jaw tight. Meeting Dorrance Lansing was more important than ever now. But the grimness stayed with him as he rode. There'd been the hint of a grin on the deputy's face, as though he were savoring some sort of victory. Fargo felt his thoughts racing and the grimness pulled itself tight around him as nasty apprehensions began to poke at him, things to which he didn't want to give definition. "Goddamn," he swore as he wheeled the horse in a tight circle and headed back the way the sheriff's men had ridden. He cut across the land at an angle to catch up to them and he was racing up a slope of barberries when he heard the single shot.

"Son of a bitch," he flung into the wind as the dread certainty swept through him. He raced over the top of the slope to see the bearded figure crumpled on the ground just ahead of him and his eyes found the river of red flowing from the man's head. He didn't pause at John Waller's figure. It was too late for that. He swerved the Ovaro as he glimpsed the horse and rider disappearing into a stand of birch and oak.

"Bastards," he shouted in fury as he sent the Ovaro racing after the fleeing rider. He plunged into the trees and glimpsed the fleeing figure again, listened for a half-second, and caught the sound of other horses racing through the woods. He concentrated on the rider in his sight and sent the Ovaro darting and swerving through narrow spaces between trees. The other horse had already slowed, the rider unable to get the sure-footed quickness out of his mount. Fargo saw the man turn to glance back at him as he closed ground. The man reined his mount to a halt and Fargo saw the glint of gunmetal as the man brought his arm up. The Trailsman continued to race forward as he flattened himself onto the Ovaro's withers and the first shot sped harmlessly over him. He swerved the horse sharply and the deputy's second shot came closer but fell wide as the Ovaro turned.

Fargo leapt from the horse as the third shot whistled through the air. He landed in a thicket of brush and, legs bent, stayed on his feet. The Colt flew into his hand as he saw the man yank his horse around to flee. Fargo's shot caught the man in the left shoulder as he tried to push between two oaks. The man cried out in pain and Fargo saw him clutch at his shoulder.

"Hold it there or you're a dead man," Fargo called. The sheriff's depty halted his horse, slowly turned as he remained in the saddle. Fargo held the Colt aimed at the man's shoulder. "Drop the gun and get down, nice and easy," he called.

The man obeyed, letting the gun fall from his hand as he slid from his horse, wincing in pain as he did. The man dropped to one knee as Fargo straightened and came toward him. "Answers, you bastard. I want to know who gave the orders," Fargo rasped.

The man nodded, still on one knee. "My shoulder hurts real bad. Can I sit?" the man asked, and Fargo nodded permission. He watched as the sheriff's deputy slid from one knee to the ground, putting his arm out to brace himself. His move was fast, a dive for the gun lying on the grass as he lowered himself within reach. Fargo saw his hand close around the weapon and the big Colt barked, an automatic, instant reaction. The man's chest blew open as the heavy slug tore into his collarbone and down through his upper chest cavity. He made a strange inhuman sound as he pitched forward to lay facedown, quickly staining the grass red.

"Goddamn stupid son of a bitch," Fargo swore as he holstered the big Colt .45 and strode to where he'd left the Ovaro. With anger a cold, grim fire inside him, he rode back to John Waller's slain form, wrapped the man's head in an old piece of shirt from his saddlebag, and draped his lifeless body over the saddle. He turned the Ovaro toward Owl Creek, riding at a funereal pace as his anger burned inside him. They had done the deed and hightailed it for safety. They'd have answers ready, of course, and he would listen to them. He could play the same game as they did. But somebody would pay, sooner or later, somebody would pay.

He reached Owl Creek still riding slowly and men stepped to one side as he moved down the center of Main Street with his lifeless burden. He spotted the four deputies outside Roy Curry's office. The sheriff was with them. Fargo moved toward them without hastening his pace.

The sheriff stepped forward to meet the big man whose eyes were the blue of ice-floes in a January lake. "Now, don't go exploding, Fargo," the sheriff said as the big man halted his horse. "My men told me John Waller changed his mind about comin' in and pulled a gun on them. They had to shoot him. Self-defense, right, Strainer?" Roy Curry said with a glance at the bulbous-nosed man. The man nodded in agreement.

Fargo's eyes bored hard into the sheriff and his words were barely audible. "Why'd they hightail it?" he asked.

"They didn't hightail it. They just rode off to get back and tell me what happened," the sheriff said. "It would never have happened if he hadn't pulled the gun on them. In fact, one of my men hasn't come back yet. You see him along the way?"

"He won't be back," Fargo said, and saw the sheriff's eyes narrow. "He pulled a gun on me. I had to shoot him. Self-defense. It would never have happened if he hadn't pulled the gun on me." Fargo saw Roy Curry's eyes flicker, but he held his tongue. "I'll take Waller to the undertaker. His wife can claim him tomorrow," Fargo said, and started to slowly walk the Ovaro on. He paused beside the man with the bulbous nose. "I'm going to do you a favor before this is over," he said. "I'm going to blow that fat nose right off your face." He rode on as the man swallowed hard.

He stopped at the town undertaker's, and then headed back out of Owl Creek as the dusk slid over the land. He had decided to put off visiting Dorrance Lansing till morning. He wanted his fury to cool down before he took on matching wits with the man. He hurried his pinto through the last light. But it was dark when he reached the Weller place and saw Bess hurry outside to greet him. He dismounted in the square of lamplight that streamed from the open doorway, and Bess searched his face, her frown beginning to dig into her brow as she picked up the unsaid words in his eyes.

"No," she breathed. "Oh, God, no." The harsh grimness in his face was her answer, and he told what had happened in short, terse sentences. She spun around when he finished, her fists beating against a fencepost. "Damn, I should never have listened to you," she half-sobbed. "Damn you, damn them, damn everything."

He let her vent her feelings and he stayed silent. They had drawn him into it in a way nothing else could, and he'd see it to the finish now. "Just leave me be," Bess said. "I'll stay the night with Harriet, probably go into Owl Creek with her, come morning."

"I'll tell the others," he said, and pulled himself onto the Ovaro. He started to ride out when she turned to call after him.

"I know you didn't think it'd turn out this way," she said, half an apology, which she pulled back just as quickly. "Doesn't change things any, though, does it?" she said.

He moved the Ovaro slowly away from the truth in her words. He headed through the valley with the moon rising to paint a silver path. A figure with a rifle stepped forward to challenge him as he reached the camp, and he recognized Kelby Joust.

"Fargo," Kelby said as he rode forward and dismounted. The small figure of Charlie Burrows appeared and Fargo told both men about John Waller.

"The bastards," Kelby Joust muttered. "I'll tell the others to make a place for Harriet and the youngsters. The Thompsons have room."

He hurried away and Fargo sat down atop a length of log. He stared into the darkness, lips pursed. Charlie Burrows slid down beside him. "You're bothered, but not just by what happened," the little man said, and drew a glance from Fargo. "You're thinking it's too bad I can't shoot as fast as I can pick up things." Charlie Burrows laughed.

"Maybe," Fargo conceded.

"Can't do much about that any longer," the little man

said, and shook his thatch of white hair. "What else is picking at you, Fargo?" he queried.

"I'm thinking they're going to a lot of trouble to wrap everything they do in the law," Fargo said. "Everything's backed by a decision by Judge Tolliver, all recorded, all in order."

"Nobody coming along later could know it was all based on lyin', schemin', and railroadin'," Charlie said bitterly.

"That's right. I'd say that means that Dorrance Lansing figures to file claims for all the lands," Fargo said. "Then, why hasn't he moved in, taken over physical possession of the lands?"

"Filing claims means going to the land-claims office in Washington. That takes time. Maybe he doesn't want to move till he's gotten all the claims on file proper," Charlie offered.

Fargo squinted back. "Possible, but it doesn't really hold. Physical possession of the lands would only help him back up the claims. Besides, a man that's hungry for land usually moves in the minute he gets the chance. Lansing's holding back. Why?" Fargo thought aloud.

"Can't say." Charlie shrugged.

"There's more," Fargo followed. "Why is he letting you all camp here together?"

"Bess says he just figures we'll all have to scatter, come winter," Charlie replied.

"I know what Bess thinks and I don't buy it. It's almost as if he's giving you a chance to fight back, and that doesn't make any goddamn sense." Fargo frowned.

"Not when you look at it that way," Charlie agreed.

"Tell me, how'd they get to Fred and Nora Thompson?" Fargo asked.

"The Thompsons went to Lansing about running a cattle trail across a quarter of his land. Lansing refused. Someone shot up Lansing's house and killed one of his men. The sheriff took Fred Thompson in for it, had a witness that saw him do it," Charlie said.

"They're big on witnesses," Fargo remarked grimly. "What about the Jousts?"

"That's one of the times they had hold of something. The Jousts and some of Lansing's men got into a shootin' match over some water rights and two of Lansing's men were killed. Naturally, the sheriff took in the Jousts and Judge Tolliver sentenced them."

"Sentenced them to hang and offered them the choice of giving up their land or the gallows," Fargo said, and the little man nodded.

"How about you, Charlie?" Fargo asked.

"I staked out this nice stretch of land and Abby Weeden came out to help with household chores. Dorrance Lansing's cowhands were used to using it as a shortcut and they wouldn't stop. When two of them were found dead on my land, the sheriff charged me with bushwhacking them. Judge Tolliver agreed with the charge."

"Ted Fuller and his sister?" Fargo asked.

"They said he shot one of Lansing's men in town over a remark passed about his sister," Charlie answered. "Hell, Ted Fuller's not the kind to start a gunfight, not that he wouldn't like to, mind you."

"But?"

"He's not got the guts for it, to my way of thinking. Ted Fuller's greedy and I don't know that I'd trust him far, but he's no face-to-face gunfighter," the little man said.

"Who saw him do it, then?"

"Nobody. It happened on the street, between two buildings, a shot and Lansing's man was dead. Ted Fuller said he didn't do it, but Judge Tolliver didn't believe him. Fuller had the bad luck to have only four bullets in his gun."

Fargo's eyes were narrowed as he thought aloud. "A pattern, with variations, and Dorrance Lansing figures in each one," he said.

"Sure, he's working it through Roy Curry and the judge," Charlie said. He rose suddenly and, standing, was hardly taller than Fargo still seated on the log. "Anything you want me to do, you just holler. I don't care what it is. I've lived a good score years," he said.

"I'll remember that," Fargo said, and watched the little man hurry away in quick, spry steps.

When Charlie Burrows vanished from sight, Fargo rose and unsaddled the pinto, taking his sleeping bag under one arm. He crossed the campgrounds and had almost reached the rear edge when a tent flap was pulled open, lamplight from within spearing out into the night. A young woman looked at him from the entranceway. She was very slender, though not tall, with a body that was wiry and sinuous, even standing still.

"I'm Thea Manning," she said. "I saw you ride in." She held the tent flap open wider. "Please come in for a minute," she said, and he ducked low to fit himself through the opening. Thea Manning let the tent flap fall back as she turned to face him, slender legs encased in tight riding jeans; she had a narrow waist and smallish breasts that nonetheless gathered themselves at the undersides to push tiny points into a tan shirt. She wore her black hair loose, almost to the shoulders, but it was her face that held him, strikingly intense, with high cheekbones, an aquiline nose, a wide mouth, and green-gray eyes that seemed to shift and intermix colors as they surveyed him. "I hope you're as good as you are good-looking," Thea Manning said almost matter-of-factly. "I hear you're going to help us."

"I'm going to try," Fargo said evenly, his eyes moving around the inside of the tent, taking in the open trunk with clothes inside it in neat stacks, the old wooden chair, and the cot to one side beside a wooden chest with pots and pans in it. Thea Manning followed his eyes and her wide mouth formed a bittersweet smile.

"Not much, but I make do. Just like the others here," she said, and pointed to one of three tarpaulins that covered the ground. "Sit down," she offered, and Fargo lowered himself to the corner of one piece of canvas. Thea Manning folded herself in place, a quick, lithe motion, as though she had no joints to get in the way. As she sat cross-legged, the smallish breasts pushed against her shirt with surprising sharpness. "I can help you more than anyone else here can," she said.

"How?" he questioned.

"Dorrance Lansing once had the hots for me. I know him better than anyone here," Thea Manning said.

"Fill me in," Fargo said.

"I didn't get here the same way the others did," she began. "I was living with Jay Crooks on the land he'd settled. Jay was twice my age and he was a good man. He asked little but somebody pleasant to have around. When Dorrance Lansing took an interest in me, I was flattered. I played his game for a while and then decided to bow out. I sent him packing."

"Why? Rich man like that?" Fargo pressed.

"I realized I didn't like him," Thea said, and her smile was full of bittersweet memories. "But he kept after me, kept chasing me. Jay got angry and, against my advice, went to have it out with Dorrance. He got himself killed trying to outgun three of Lansing's hands." She drew a deep sigh from inside her, and Fargo watched the way the smallish breasts seemed to grow larger. "I got a visit from Roy Curry soon after. He had a piece of paper signed by Judge Tolliver telling me to clear off the land. I'd no right to stay on, it said. I was a girlfriend, not a wife. I realized I'd no chance, actually or legally, so I left.

I'm sure Dorrance enjoyed his revenge for being turned down."

"Why'd you stay on here with the others?" Fargo asked.

"Jay wanted me to have the land. He'd said it often enough. I've more right than Dorrance Lansing to it, so I stayed on here with the others. I want that land back. Now, with you, maybe I've a chance to get it back." Thea leaned forward, her slender body swaying as a reed in the wind. "I can help you. I know how Dorrance Lansing thinks. I know his ways, the things he'd do and not do. He talked a lot to me."

"Seems you sure could help," Fargo said.

"We can work together," Thea said, and something in the gray-green eyes caught at him.

"How close together?" He grinned.

"That depends." Thea shrugged. "Maybe very close." She rose suddenly with a sinuous effortlessness, like a winter jasmine unfolding, the gray-green eyes shifting colors. "Good night, Fargo," she said, and he pushed himself to his feet. She seemed even smaller, suddenly, but with a strength to her slender, small-waisted form.

"I look forward to it," he said.

"Working together or working close together?" Thea Manning smiled.

"Both," he said as he pushed his way through the tent flap and out into the night. He took his bedroll to the far edge of the camp, undressed, and stretched out in his shorts, the night warm and soft. He smiled as he recalled Bess's remarks about Thea, very understandable now. They were very different types. The smile clung for another moment. Perhaps he'd be doing a little juggling along with his other task. He closed his eyes and the smile faded from his lips. He slept with the tragic mistake of the day an unwelcome companion.

When morning came, he rose and washed at a small

stream behind the camp. When he finished buttoning his shirt and started toward the camp, the nervous figure of Ted Fuller stepped in front of him, the man's mouth twitching. Fargo halted, and Mary Fuller appeared from behind her brother, the subdued, almost cowed manner still part of her, he noted. "I want to talk private, Fargo," Ted Fuller said.

"I'll be back later," Fargo answered.

"All right, I'll watch for you," Ted Fuller said, and strode away. Mary Fuller hurried after her brother, but Fargo caught the quick, furtive glance she threw back at him. He began to saddle the Ovaro as Nora Thompson passed with a cheerful greeting and he saw Thea Manning step from her tent with a basketful of clothes. She wore a white shirt rolled up in halter-top fashion that exposed the deeply tanned, perfectly flat abdomen, a well-muscled lower back, and the beautiful narrow waist. She strung a clothesline and he watched as she began to hang garments. Bending, turning, leaning, stretching, each movement was fluid, almost dancelike in its sinuous grace. He returned to saddling the Ovaro only when she finished and disappeared back into her tent. A tiny little hint of a smile on her lips had been the only hint that she knew he was watching her.

Finished saddling the horse, Fargo rode out of the camp; he saw Charlie Burrows leaning against a tree and decided that those bright, snapping eyes missed little, if anything. He left the campgrounds and had almost reached the other end of the valley on his way to the double elm when he saw the cloud of dust rising into the air, then the lone rider galloping toward him. The blue-checked shirt took on its pattern and he shifted direction to meet her. Bess shouted words before she came to a halt. "They arrested Harriet, damn them," she said. "I went to Owl Creek with her to claim John's body and they arrested her."

"What the hell for?" Fargo frowned.

"Being an accessory to cattle rustling," Bess said. "That's what Roy Curry told me. She's going in front of Judge Tolliver in an hour."

"Let's go," Fargo said, his jaw tightening. The meeting with Dorrance Lansing was beginning to seem an impossible goal. He frowned.

"You get her out of there if you have to shoot every last one of them," Bess bit out in fury.

"We'll see where they go with this," Fargo said.

"You saw where they went with John," Bess snapped. "Wasn't that enough for you?"

"Making a stupid move won't help her or you and the others," Fargo said. "Now be quiet and ride."

Bess glared at him as he sent the Ovaro into a full gallop and left her behind. She didn't catch up until he reached Owl Creek and reined up in front of the courtroom. She hurried inside with him.

He swept the room with a quick glance. Roy Curry and three of his deputies were seated, one the man with the bulbous nose. A half-dozen onlookers had taken places, and as he sat down, Fargo saw Judge Tolliver emerge from the adjoining room, his hollowed, gaunt face held in dignified severity as befits a judge. Fargo saw the man's eyes spot him and look quickly away. Another of Roy Curry's men brought Harriet out of the room and walked her to stand in front of Judge Tolliver.

"Now, this here is an unpleasant task for me, Mrs. Waller," the judge began, and let stern sympathy infuse the gaunt face.

"My John was murdered. Why aren't you trying his murderers?" Harriet interrupted.

"I've sworn statements that say that your husband pulled a gun on the deputies," Judge Tolliver said.

"Sworn lies," Harriet snapped, her tone lifelessly flat.

"I'm not here to listen to your accusations. I'm here to consider your part in the original charge, Mrs. Waller." The judge frowned.

"You've all done everything you can to me. You took my husband," Harriet said in her flat, toneless voice.

"You were there when the cattle were found on your land," Judge Tolliver went on. "I can't believe your husband could rustle cattle and you not know about it, and that makes you what we call an accessory," he said.

"Say whatever you like about me. I don't care," Harriet answered.

"The bastard," Fargo heard Bess hiss in his ear.

"I've got to pass sentence on you," the judge said to the woman in front of him.

"You can't hurt me anymore," Harriet said.

Fargo saw Judge Tolliver let stern righteousness infuse his gaunt face. "I'm most bothered by you bringing up two youngsters in an atmosphere of crime and criminal behavior. This court has to be concerned for their welfare. I'm afraid it's my duty to have these children taken from you on account of your being an unfit mother."

Fargo felt Bess dig fingernails into his arm and he cursed silently as Harriet Waller's scream resounded through the room. The bastard had hit the one place he could reach her.

"No, no, you can't," he saw Harriet Waller scream and rush toward the judge only to be pulled back by the deputy at her side. "You can't do that. You wouldn't," Harriet screamed again.

"Dammit, Fargo, shoot that slimy bastard," Bess hissed.

"Be quiet," Fargo said. "That'd get a half-dozen innocent people killed in here." His eyes stayed on Judge Tolliver and he saw the man let his lips purse, an expression of pained tolerance come into his face. "Here it comes," Fargo growled at Bess.

"I could suspend signing such an order if you promise to leave here and take those children out of that climate of disregard for the law," the judge said with studied thoughtfulness.

"Yes, all right, whatever you say," Harriet answered, panic turning her voice into broken sobs.

Judge Tolliver let himself look pained and severe. "That means you give up your land and go with the children, you understand?" he intoned.

"Yes, I understand. Just don't take the children from me," Harriet pleaded.

"All right, I'll suspend the order," the judge sighed as he rose to his feet. The bastard was a good actor, Fargo swore silently. The judge gestured to the deputy. "Bring her to my chambers and I'll get the proper papers ready," he said, and strode away with his tattered black frock coat flapping behind him.

Fargo felt Bess's eyes boring into him.

"You just going to sit there?" she bit out.

"No, I'm going outside," he answered, and got to his feet. He strode from the courtroom and heard her footsteps running after him as he reached the hitching post outside. Fury wreathed her round, pugnacious face and deep breaths pushed her breasts tight against the shirt. "Rotten but clever," Fargo said. "He hit her in the one place he knew would get to her. Everything all wrapped up neat and legal again."

"I don't care about that. I want them stopped," Bess snapped. "I'm going to help Harriet take her things to the camp. You coming?" she snapped.

"No. Got other plans," he told her, and she stared in disapproval and annoyance at him as she led her horse away. He climbed onto the Ovaro, his thoughts still on the charade he had just witnessed. All their careful attention to legal chicanery still left too much unexplained. Too many things still didn't fit right, refused to make sense. It was time for a visit with Dorrance Lansing.

4

The ranch house was impressive, fieldstone and logs, barns behind it with corrals spreading out and plenty of shade trees nearby. Fargo halted as he came into view of the spread just over the top of a low slope, and he saw the three riders appear and converge to cut in front of him as he rode closer to the house. "I'm expected," he said as he reined up before the three cowhands. "Skye Fargo," he added.

The three men moved back and he rode through, halted outside the main house, and slid from the saddle as a man emerged to walk quickly almost enthusiastically, toward him.

"Dorrance Lansing," the man said, and Fargo felt the surprise push at him from inside himself. He had expected someone commanding, perhaps abrasive, a man whose face would mirror the ruthlessness and cruelty behind it. But Dorrance Lansing seemed none of those things as Fargo took in a bland face, very blond hair, thick and tumbling casually over his forehead, handsome in an overblown way with jowls a little large, cheeks a little soft, blue eyes a little weak. He saw self-indulgence, not strength, in Dorrance Lansing's face, weakness more than ruthlessness. Of course, he reminded himself, weakness could be deceptive and self-indulgence could easily slip into cruelty. "Come in, Fargo, come in. Been waiting for you," Dorrance Lansing said expansively as he led the way into the house.

Fargo found himself inside a large room, a combination living room and study, richly furnished with fine, dark-wood furniture, the walls hung with furs and skins. Wide, thick oak beams crossed the ceiling and a heavy wooden desk took up one corner of the room. Solid chairs and a round, low table occupied the center.

"Please sit down, Fargo," Dorrance Lansing said. "I'm glad Sheriff Curry was able to give you my message."

Fargo eased himself into one of the solid chairs and noted that Lansing was a large man, maybe fifteen pounds overweight, but large-boned under the fat. "The sheriff talked. I listened," Fargo said.

Dorrance Lansing's smile was quick and smooth. "You're not impressed with Roy," he said.

"That about fits it," Fargo remarked.

"Roy told me how you got involved helping some of the valley people," Lansing said.

"Guess I did," Fargo allowed.

Dorrance Lansing's smile was laced with ruefulness. "You figured you were doing right," he said. "Anyone can make a mistake."

"Is that what I did, make a mistake?" Fargo inquired.

"Yes," Dorrance Lansing said at once.

Fargo picked out words. "They seem to think differently," he observed.

"I've given up trying to understand those people," Lansing said as he pushed his thick blond hair back, and his tone seemed almost petulant.

"What don't you understand about them?" Fargo asked casually.

Lansing's eyes flashed back and the petulance was in his voice again. "My men are killed, my cattle stolen, my barns burned, and they go around posing as victims, blaming me for it," he said.

"They seem to think you set up all those incidents so the sheriff and Judge Tolliver could follow through," Fargo probed.

"Of course they'd say that," Dorrance Lansing returned. "Sheriff Curry and Judge Tolliver are only trying to bring some law into the region."

Fargo nodded at the man's answers. They were no more than he'd expected, neat, glib, turn-away answers, and yet there was something more, something he couldn't define yet.

Lansing interrupted his thoughts. "But I didn't ask you here to talk about those miserable valley people. I want to show you something," the man said, and Fargo watched him stride to the desk, open a top drawer, and pull out a folded square of heavy paper. He returned to Fargo and spread the piece of paper out on the round table, where it became a crude but unmistakable map. "Black Canyon, Fargo. You know where that is?" Lansing asked.

"Just a few miles north of the valley," Fargo said.

"Exactly," Lansing said, and jabbed a finger at the map. "And fifty thousand dollars in silver is sitting there, waiting for me, practically under my nose. I've a map, marked, the real thing, and I can't find the goddamn silver." He pushed the map at Fargo again. "This is the original, but I've two copies I had made, exactly like it. It's marked clear enough, isn't it?" he demanded.

Fargo scanned the map, crude but simple, natural landmarks noted, trails drawn in. "Seems clear enough," he said.

"Then why can't I find it?" Lansing exploded.

"I take it you looked," Fargo said.

"I looked, but I'm no good at that kind of thing," Lansing said quickly. "That's why I asked Roy to get hold of you when I heard you were in town. You're the very best, I hear. You see where other's only look. I want you to find the silver for me. Five hundred now, ten percent of whatever's there when you find it. That'll be a lot of money, Fargo."

"It will be," Fargo agreed. "But maybe you didn't find it because it's not there."

"It's there," Dorrance Lansing said. "The lifetime work of an old prospector. He buried it over a period of forty years, then dropped dead before he had a chance to enjoy it."

"How do you know all this?" Fargo questioned.

"He was a friend of my pa, and when he was dyin', he gave Pa the map," Lansing said. "Pa used to stake him on some of his digs. It's there, believe me. You just find it and make yourself some real money."

Fargo let his thoughts race as the man waited eagerly. The offer was unexpected, unusual, and on the surface, too goddamn transparent. Unless Dorrance Lansing was a completely unsubtle fool. It was too soon to discount anything, but if the man were playing a game, he'd picked one that could backfire, Fargo pondered silently. He let his glance go to Dorrance Lansing and saw the eager waiting in the man's eyes. "Five hundred up front?" he asked.

Dorrance Lansing's eyes lighted as he strode to the desk, pulled a drawer open, and rolled a tight wad of bills across the desk. "Up front enough?" Lansing said.

Fargo let them lie there. "I take this on, I want to be free to come and go. I want to come back here and ask more questions, or just bed down; I don't want to be hassled by your boys," he said. "I don't want to have to explain anything to anybody but you."

"You've my word on it. I'll tell them you're working for me. Nobody'll bother you," Lansing said.

Fargo picked up the roll of bills and stuffed them into his shirt pocket. "If it's there, I'll find it," he said. "Let me have the map."

Lansing reached into another drawer in the desk and brought out a copy, and Fargo scanned it against the original. It was identical and he put it into his pocket. "I'll report back after I look around some," he said as he headed for the door.

Lansing's smile was expansive as he pushed the thick blond hair from his forehead. "I feel good about this. I know you'll find it, Fargo," he called as Fargo went out to the Ovaro and swung onto the horse. He let another slow glance print the layout of Dorrance Lansing's spread in his mind as he rode off, three of Lansing's men watching him with curiosity. He rode slowly, turned the Ovaro to head for the valley.

It had been a strange turn of events, Fargo mused, an offer that seemed too obvious and a man that didn't fit the picture of clever ruthlessness. He let his thoughts speculate until he grew annoyed and pushed them all aside. It was too early for speculation; too many things didn't make sense. He'd have to wait till he had something more to cling to, and he thought about Thea Manning. Perhaps she could fill in some of the holes, and he quickened the Ovaro's pace.

But the night blanketed the land before he reached the end of the valley and he saw the cooking fires burning in the campground as he rode in. Ned and Ruth Simmons were the first to offer him a plate of grits, and he sat down among the others around the fire. He saw Bess helping Harriet Waller move a wooden chest into the Thompsons' tent, and he waited till they finished and sat down in front of the fire before he rose to his feet as the cooking fires began to burn down. "Got a new job today," he announced as his glance swept the circle of faces. "Working for Dorrance Lansing," he said.

The collective gasp rippled through the night and he scanned the eyes that stared at him, most with frowns, Bess with shocked disbelief, and Thea Manning with the hint of a smile on her wide mouth. He told them of his visit to Lansing and the job he'd been offered and had taken, recounting the meeting just as it had taken place.

Bess was first to respond when he finished, her voice bristling with anger. "He only hired you to get you out of his hair and to keep tabs on you," she snapped out. "It's as plain as the nose on your face, dammit."

"Maybe too plain," Fargo said calmly.

"Meaning what?" Bess returned sharply.

"Meaning if that's why he did it, I'm on to that game, and watching is a two-way street," Fargo said.

"He's not going to let you spy on him," she retorted. "He's going to expect you to spend your time in Black Canyon. He'll probably have someone watching you."

"That'll be my problem. But this lets me come and go at his place and that's important. If it lets him think he's got me under his thumb, so much the better for it," Fargo answered.

"I can't see how it does us any harm," Charlie Burrows put in.

"Me neither," Ollie Joust said. "It's sort of turning his own game around on him."

"I don't like it," Bess glowered stubbornly.

"I think it's a perfectly wonderful idea," Thea Manning said. "Of course, Fargo will be taking all the chances."

Fred Thompson's voice chimed in. "You think it'll help you nail Dorrance Lansing, Fargo, I'm all for it," the man said, and was followed by a chorus of agreement.

Fargo found Bess's eyes, saw no concession in their

glower. "Just wanted everybody to know," he said to the others.

"Be careful. Don't underestimate any of them," Abby Weeden warned as the cooking fires burned themselves out. The others rose to start to clean dishes and return to their tents and huts.

Fargo picked up his bedroll and started across the camp with it. He caught Ted Fuller's eyes following him as he walked to the far edge of the camp and laid out his bedroll. He folded himself on the blanket and waited the visit from Ted Fuller with impatience. He had a visit of his own to pay, and he rose when Ted Fuller appeared, the man's mouth twitching nervously. Something suddenly weasellike about Ted Fuller struck at him, more than the man's nervous twitch.

"Speak your piece," he growled.

Ted Fuller's eyes grew smaller. "I've some extra money put away. It's yours if you want it," he said. Fargo's face remained expressionless as his eyes speared the man in front of him. "I just want some special attention," Ted Fuller said. "You make a special try at getting proof that Lansing railroaded me. I want my land back."

"So do the others," Fargo commented.

"The hell with the others. You concentrate on proof Lansing railroaded me, first," Ted Fuller said harshly.

"I thought you were all pulling together in this," Fargo questioned.

"Sure, but a man's got to look out for himself," Fuller said.

"I've heard that excuse before," Fargo commented.

"What're you saying?" the man asked.

"I'm saying nobody gets special treatment," Fargo answered.

"It's a good piece of extra money, Fargo," Ted Fuller said.

"Not interested," Fargo said.

Fuller's darting eyes slowed enough to study the Trailsman for a moment. "Maybe money doesn't mean that much to you," he said.

"Maybe not," Fargo said. "Now get out of here."

Ted Fuller stayed a half-second more and then the man walked away. When he vanished into the dark, Fargo took a sip of water from his canteen to wash away the sour taste in his mouth. He straightened his bedroll and headed for Thea Manning's tent, off to the other side of the grounds.

The tent flap pulled open as he reached it. "Come on in," she said, her intense, thin face catching a tiny smile. "I expected you'd be coming with questions."

"You said we'd work close together," he reminded her, and her little smile widened.

"So I did," she answered, and let the tent flap fall shut as he entered. She wore a man's shirt that hung down to her knees and she sank onto a large mat spread over the ground. She moved with an effortless gracefulness that let him glimpse long, thin calves in the soft light of the kerosene lamp turned low. She reached under a small mound of clothes and brought out a jug. "Kentucky rye," she said, pulling the stopper from the jug.

"Why not?" Fargo smiled as she handed him the jug. He lifted it to his lips and let the warm dark liquid slide down his throat, breath-catching and invigorating at the same time. "Good whiskey," he commented, and watched her drink from the jug. She tilted her head way back and the loose shirt pulled tight against the smallish breasts, outlining their tiny tips with surprising deliciousness. She lowered the jug, put the stopper back in place, and leaned on her elbows, green-gray eyes regarding him with quiet amusement.

"Start asking," Thea Manning said.

"He ever talk about the silver to you?" Fargo questioned.

"Lots of times," Thea said, and Fargo felt a twinge of surprise.

"Then he really thinks it's there." Fargo frowned.

"He's sure of it," Thea said. "He tell you he hired two others before you to find it?"

The surprise became more than a twinge. "No." Fargo frowned. "Two together or one at a time?" he asked.

"One at a time," Thea said.

"They didn't find anything, I take it," Fargo said.

"Not that I know of," Thea said. "Dorrance was still talking about finding the silver when he was chasing after me."

"He send them packing when they didn't come up with anything?" Fargo queried.

"Guess so." She shrugged. "He never exactly said so to me, though." Fargo frowned into space as he turned Thea's words in his mind. "What are you thinking?" Thea asked.

"It's become plain that he didn't invent this to keep me busy and out of his way, but maybe he saw a chance to kill two birds with one stone," Fargo said.

Thea's laugh was soft. "I like you, Fargo. You don't sell anyone short," she said.

"I try not to," he said. Thea Manning leaned back farther and the shirt rode up higher, to reveal thin knees and a long, slender thigh. "How'd Lansing get to be so rich?" Fargo asked. "He make it himself?"

"No, his pa left him rich," she said.

Fargo nodded. "Figured maybe that was it," he murmured.

"Why'd you ask that?" Thea questioned, green-gray eyes amused.

"Helps fill in a picture," he said.

"What sort of a picture?"

"Tell you more when I've decided more." He smiled.

"Any more questions?" she asked, half-turned, and the smallish breasts pressed against the shirt at one side.

"Not now, not about Lansing," Fargo said.

The amusement stayed in the green-gray eyes. "About anything else?" she murmured.

"How about Thea Manning?" Fargo said, and he leaned toward her. She didn't move and he saw her eyes turn green. Her lips came open just a fraction, but it was enough and he pressed his mouth on hers. She didn't pull away and he pressed down harder, let his tongue slide over her lips. He felt her mouth widen and her hands came up to dig into his shoulders. She pulled back, her eyes searching his face.

"Questions come with words," Thea said.

"Not always," he answered, and she half-shrugged, opened her lips, and lifted her mouth to his. He let his tongue press forward into the warmth of her mouth and she gave a tiny shudder. He heard her words in the spaces between her answering kisses. "Forgotten how good it feels," she breathed.

He paused and drew back, and she pushed herself to a sitting position. Her fingers pulled at the buttons on the shirt; she wriggled her shoulders, and the shirt fell from her. His eyes moved over her supple, beautifully thin, yet perfectly proportioned shape; square shoulders, prominent collarbones, her back curving to a tiny waist. She rose to her knees before him, and naked, the small-ish breasts didn't seem small at all but perfect on the supple, sinuous body, twin brown-pink points thrusting up sharply.

He let his eye move down across the flatness of her belly, a tight body with not an extra ounce of flesh on it, and below her flat little belly a tangled, bushy, dense triangle, a veritable forest that grew up past the pubic mound, over the edge of her little belly, and extended its fuzzy edges along the inside of her thighs. Strangely exciting, its black tangled denseness was a luxuriant invitation.

Thea leaned toward him and he shed his clothes. He reached out as her hands grasped his bare shoulders and ran down his chest, palms pressed flat against him. He saw her eyes widen as she glanced down at the size of him. "Oh, Jesus," she breathed, and fell into him. Her arms encircled his neck and he felt her legs come up, long and wiry, clasping him around the waist. "Oh, Christ, Fargo, take me, Jesus, take me," she cried out, and her mouth was harsh, demanding, and thirsting against his. He felt her legs pull away, straighten, and move to rub up and down his body, over his swelling maleness. He found one breast in his mouth, sucked deeply, and pulled on it until Thea cried out and rubbed her legs frantically up and down his body. He felt her torso twist and turn, serpentlike, her body writhing around his as her hands fluttered up and down his ribs.

Every part of her seemed to entwine, press, and want. From her lips came soft, breathy little cries. He pressed his hand onto her abdomen and she fell from him onto her back at once. "Yes, oh, Jesus, yes, Fargooooo . . . oooh, now, oh, now," Thea Manning cried out, and he moved his fingers down into the luxuriant, profuse, dense black tangle, and rubbed her, letting the wiry-soft hairs brush against his probing hand. He reached down farther and found her thighs moist as they parted at once for him. Her warm darkness was wet, flowing with desire. He felt her hand reach down and seize him, roughly, harshly. She lifted her legs, and spread them wider as she gasped hoarse little sounds. "Please, please, Jesus God, please," Thea half-sobbed. He lay over her, letting his pulsating desire slide into the wet warmth that waited hungrily, and Thea screamed, satisfaction and pleasure laced together in the sound. Her long, thin thighs moved up and down his hips, rubbing, tightening, then rubbing again even as her dense, tangled nap came up to press against him. Her entire supple, sinuous body writhed as she pumped with him.

He felt her knees draw up and press into the sides of his ribs as she strove to take in all of him, and he heard the little cry of ecstasy as his organ pressed against the very end of her wet, warm funnel. He swallowed one little breast, played with it inside his mouth. "Ah . . . ah, ah, ah," Thea gasped out, and he felt her legs suddenly fall away from him, stay still for a brief moment, and clasp back around him with renewed fervor. The slender, supple body began to quiver as it writhed, and he saw Thea Manning's eyes grow wide, stare at him, deep, dark green, and her mouth fell open.

"Coming . . . Jesus, I'm coming. Oh, Christ, Fargo . . . oh, please, come with me . . . come, come . . . oh, Jesus," she screamed against him, and he drew back for a moment and her scream turned to panic until he thrust forward. She cried out, her fingers digging into his shoulders, and he heard the scream gather inside her, felt her flat belly thrust upward. He let her begin to explode before he joined her, and when he did, with a final, frenzied motion, Thea Manning all but slid out from under him as she pulled and thrust and rubbed her legs wildly against him. Her screams were gasped sounds against his chest.

The moment that was never long enough spiraled away. Thea shuddered as he lay atop her, still inside her. Slowly, her legs began moving up and down his powerful thighs, lifting, rubbing against his ribs, pressing into his hips, then straightening to move against his legs. "Oh, my God, my God," Thea breathed as she took her arms from around his neck; her eyes were green-gray again, he saw, as she looked up at him. The tiny smile touched the corners of her wide mouth and her high-cheekboned, strikingly attractive face seemed to glow in the dim light of the lamp. She drew a deep sigh, but her legs continued to rub up and down his body, against his buttocks, over his hips, and down along his powerful thighs. It seemed to be a reflex action, a thing all its own, hardly a part of her.

"Been a long time, I'd say," Fargo ventured.

"Too long," Thea Manning murmured. "But you were worth the waiting."

"I can't bow from this position." Fargo grinned.

"I knew it'd be something special with you from the moment I saw you," she said, and he caressed one lovely little breast with his thumb. She grasped his hand, pressed it over her breast, and a small sound of pleasure escaped her lips. Her legs continued to rub up and down against him, strangely soothing, and he felt the thick bushy forest of her triangle against his pelvis. "We must keep working close together," she murmured.

"Sure thing," he agreed; she stretched and he felt her legs drop away, grow still beneath him. Her finger traced idly along his arm, halted as it came to the half-moon scar. She questioned with a glance of the green-gray eyes. "She-grizzly," he said. "I was lucky that's all she left with me."

Thea Manning smiled. "Only female you probably really remember," she said, and he heard his laugh as he moved to lie beside her. She wasn't all that far from the truth, he admitted silently. The kerosene lamp had burned almost to the wick, he saw.

"Time to go," he said.

"Get some more questions together," Thea said as he rose and began to pull on clothes.

"You can count on it." He grinned down at her.

Her little smile was its own answer. "I meant for real," she said. "I can help you nail them."

"I'm sure of it," Fargo said. "Maybe I'll have some more to ask you about tomorrow."

"Not tomorrow. I'm going to Saddle Rock. With Harriet Waller and her youngsters here, they'll be needing a stock of supplies," Thea said. "It's a good haul. I'll be back by the next day, though."

She pulled the tent flap open as she stood to one side, looking suddenly very small in her nakedness but also perfectly balanced in her tight-bodied, sinuous suppleness. She blew him a kiss as he left and let the tent flap close at once.

Fargo walked slowly across the dark, silent campground to where he'd left his bedroll. Thea had been of help already, in big ways and in little ones. She'd be of more help, he was certain. And of more pleasure. It was a combination to make him optimistic. He had just reached the bedroll when a figure stepped from the shadows, its round, pugnacious face burning with anger.

"Damn you, Fargo," Bess hissed. "You don't waste any time, do you?" He met her furious glare in silence. "I came looking for you earlier. I only waited to tell you I won't be coming again."

"Simmer down," he said quietly. "I didn't plan anything. Things happen."

Bess's eyes flashed. "You couldn't wait for me?"

"Didn't expect you," he said.

"Think of a better excuse," she flung back.

"Fate," he said, and couldn't stop the smile that edged his lips. "You know, things that are meant to happen."

"Bastard," Bess spit out.

"What's the matter? Doesn't fate apply to other women?" he speared.

"Go to hell," she said as she stalked away.

He watched her storm into a tent and emerge moments later, carrying her saddle. "What're you doing with that?" he asked as he stepped forward.

"Going back to my place," she snapped.

"Hell you are," he answered. "Roy Curry will have his boys checking on your place."

"He wants my pa, not me," she said.

"He'll be happy to get you. Right now they can't move against your land legally and *legal*'s the key word with them. But if they get rid of you, what with your pa being a fugitive, the good judge can declare your land vacated all nice and legal," Fargo said.

"I can take care of myself," Bess glowered.

Fargo snorted derisively. "Hell, you can't even take care of the jealousy you've no call to have," he said. She tried to brush past him, but he stopped her with an upraised arm. "Do I have to hog-tie you?" he growled.

She glared, well aware it was no idle threat. "No," she capitulated, and turned back to the tent with the saddle.

"I've got your word?" Fargo pressed.

She cast him a glance. "Yes, damn you," she said and pushed her way back into the tent.

He heard her drop the saddle on the ground, and walked to his bedroll, undressed, and settled down. He turned off thoughts of warm, hungry women and jealous girls, and slept.

5

Black Canyon was only a few miles directly north of the valley, a place of narrow passages, gnarled, twisted stone, and wind-bent trees that clung precariously in the hostile environment of cliffs. Through the center of it the Gunnison River leapt its way along a twisting, rock strewn path.

Fargo's eyes scanned the forbidding stone walls as he rode. He'd risen with the dawn, left the camp still asleep, and now he took the first path that led upward into the towering rock formations.

The map marked a second path that cut off from the first, and he followed it through a narrow pass of sheer stone that rose steeply. He rode higher and still higher, and the canyon rocks continued to rise above him. The river was already far below him, a white-flecked thread as it raced over jagged rocks. Some of the rock rose in gray-white granite, some in red clay, but the walls were mostly of black and dark-gray stone that gave the canyon its name. As he continued up through the passage that led between the black walls, he pulled the map from his pocket and scanned it again. Folding it away, he spurred the Ovaro upward as his gaze swept the higher rock formations until he found what the map had marked, two black cones that spiraled up side by side.

He found another narrow passageway that brought him to the twin slabs of rock, and he followed the wider passageway behind the rock formation that the map had shown. The pass rose on one side in a wall of rough-textured black stone and fell away on the other side to let him see the river far below. The land became a high chasm and his eyes peered at the ground. Mostly stone and hardened clay, with a few patches of scrub brush, it revealed nothing. He felt the perspiration trickling down his chest as the sun blazed down and reflected from the rocks to turn the canyon into a searing, enervating furnace. He rested the pinto for a few minutes and unbuttoned his shirt. He peered down over the edge of the gorge. The racing river was too far below to send up any cooling spray, and he rode on, the map in his hand again.

According to the map, he was on the right pathway, though he was far from certain with the number of small passages that wound through the stone walls, some little more than crevices. He rode slowly as the sun continued to sear and the passageway climbed higher, bordered the deep chasm until it emerged onto a flat circle of land surrounded mostly by black rock with some gray-white granite. In startling contrast to the rest, an area of hard, red clay spiraled at one side and slid down to form a series of thick, uneven mounds at the base at the other side.

Fargo pulled the map open again. The top of the spiral of red clay was clearly the place marked with a large *X* on the map, and he dismounted to pull himself up on foot until he was atop the thick, wide spiral. He saw the marks of digging, the ridges of shovels, and the sharp indentations of pickaxes, the almost solid, dry clay broken into deep gouges. He knelt and drew his fingers over the red clay, pushed against the broken edges. Someone had dug deep into the spiral of hard, sunbaked clay where it flattened out at the top, but he saw no signs of anything having been unearthed. It was impossible to be certain, but the dry, hard clay seemed simply broken up and gouged out in a random pattern. There was no hole that seemed large enough to remove anything.

He glanced at the map again. This was unquestionably the place marked, and he climbed around to the other side of the spiral of red clay where it bordered the black rock. It was smooth, the wall curving downward to the uneven mounds at the base. All the digging had been at the flat top of the spiral and he slid down to rest in the shadow of a wall of granite. He wiped his brow with the sleeve of his shirt. Digging here would have to be done in the late afternoon, when the sun took its blistering, direct rays toward the horizon. Or by lamplight at night.

One of the two men Thea had told him about had to have found the spot, Fargo pondered. Maybe both had, and another question pushed itself forward at once. The place had been easy to find with the map in hand. Why hadn't Lansing uncovered it himself? Fargo frowned. New questions to add to the others. He pushed himself to his feet. It was time to lean a little more on Dorrance Lansing. Perhaps he'd underestimated the man's deviousness, he reckoned as he mounted the Ovaro and began the slow, careful ride down the narrow, precipitous passages of Black Canyon.

The sun continued to bake the tall rock formations with reflected heat, and Fargo rode slowly, pausing to rest the horse often. The morning had gone into afternoon when he reached the bottom of the canyon. He gratefully welcomed the lush greenery of the valley. He rode into the campground to let the Ovaro drink from the stream before going on to meet Lansing. He saw Charlie Burrows coming toward him, the little figure moving in quick, spry steps. "If you're looking for Bess Hanford, she's gone," the little man said.

"Gone where?" Fargo frowned.

"Back to her place," Charlie Burrows said.

"Damn her hide," Fargo exploded.

"She said to tell you the promise was for last night only," Charlie said.

"Damn fool girl," Fargo said as he swung onto the Ovaro and sent the pinto into a fast canter. He cursed to himself as he headed down the center of the valley until he had almost reached the other end, where he turned and neared the Hanford cabin. He halted on a low hill that let him look down at the cabin, his eyes searching instantly for Bess's brown mare. The horse wasn't there and his jaw tightened as he sent the Ovaro down to the cabin. The cabin door hung open and Fargo halted, his eyes on the ground. She had been there; there were fresh hoofprints of a horse tethered to the hitching post. But she'd had company—three other horses had halted near the hitching post, he saw. His eyes went to the loose soil outside the cabin door. She'd been dragged out to her horse. His eyes were narrow as he followed the prints from the cabin.

He turned the Ovaro and moved after the hoofprints, which led up the north slope of the valley. The tree cover thickened the slope, but the trail was fresh, not more than a half-hour old, he estimated, the marks in the dirt still moist.

He picked his way through chestnut, birch, and alder and had reached the top of the slope when he heard a sharp scream and then sobbing. He shifted direction and pushed through thick holly-leaved buckthorn. He halted as he heard the voices over the sobbing, and slid noiselessly from the saddle to move forward, pausing to pull the big Sharps from its saddle holster.

Pushing through the thick green of the tall buckthorn,

the figures came into view in a small glen. Bess, stripped naked, lay across a log on her stomach, bound hand and foot, her round little rear pushing into the air. He drew his lips back in disgust as he saw two broad red welts across her back. His eyes went to the three men: two standing back, and the third one, the man the sheriff had called Strainer, nearest Bess, his big, bulbous nose red. He held a wide belt with a buckle in one hand and a quirt in the other. Fargo saw the angry, narrow stripes of the quirt across the back of the girl's legs.

"Don't know . . . don't know," Fargo heard Bess sob, her head over the other side of the log, her face pressed into the grass.

"Your pa told you where he was going," Strainer said. "He wouldn't ride off and not tell you a thing."

"He did," Bess gasped. "I don't know anything."

"I'm going to have to beat you some more, honey, 'less you tell me the truth," the man said.

"I don't know, I don't know," Bess said, her voice muffled into the grass.

Fargo saw the man move a step closer to the naked form across the log, take a fresh grip on the wide belt in his one hand. He started to raise his arm. Fargo brought the rifle to his shoulder, let the man's big, bulbous nose fill the rifle sight. He pressed the trigger, the Sharps fired, and Strainer's entire nose vanished in an explosion of flesh, bone, and blood.

The man screamed as blood poured from the hole in the center of his face. He fell to his knees in agony. "Jesus—ow, Christ," Strainer screamed again, but his screams had already started to become gargling sounds as blood poured down his face and into his mouth. He brought his hands to his face only to pull them away instantly, and he pitched forward, rolled onto his back, his knees drawn up. He made gurgling sounds as his lifeblood spurted out of his face as though it were being pumped upward.

The other two men had frozen, transfixed by the sickening sight. When they recovered from their surprise, one started to yank his gun from its holster. Fargo fired the big Sharps again and the man flew backward, both hands clutched to his midsection. He hit against a birch and crumpled to the ground, hands still clasped to his abdomen, but now they had suddenly turned red.

Fargo saw the third man dive into the brush, and held back a third shot as the man's heels disappeared behind the foliage.

Strainer continued to roll on the ground, but he had clapped both hands to his face despite the pain in a fruitless effort to hold back the river of red that poured from where his nose had been.

Fargo heard the shout from behind the bushes across from him.

"You just goin' to let him bleed to death in front of you?" the man called.

"Depends," Fargo said over Strainer's gargled moans. "You come out with your hands up and you can help him."

The man waited and Fargo knew he was weighing his options. "I'm coming out," he heard the third man say, and saw the figure push from the brush, hands atop his head.

"Throw your gun into the bushes, nice and easy," Fargo ordered, and watched the man comply before he straightened and stepped into the clear space, the rifle aimed at the man's gut. Fargo nodded at Strainer's quivering, bleeding figure. "He's all yours. Take him back to the sheriff," he said.

The man rushed to the figure on the ground, tore Strainer's shirt from him, and pressed it into the spurting hole, then tied it around his head. He half-carried, half-dragged Strainer to his horse, pushed him onto the saddle, and climbed on behind him.

"If he makes it, get him a smaller nose," Fargo said.

The man shot a glance at him that held hate and awe in it as he rode away.

Fargo knelt beside the log and used his throwing knife to cut Bess free. He lifted her carefully and she swayed against him as she regained her feet, her round face drawn tight in pain. "You're in no condition for me to tell you what I'm thinking," Fargo growled. "But you can be damn sure I will tomorrow." He led her to the brown mare.

"My clothes," she muttered.

"Lie across the saddle on your stomach," he told her, and boosted her onto the horse. When she was draped crosswise across the saddle, he placed her clothes carefully over her bleeding, raw welts, tied the garments so they'd stay in place, and swung onto the Ovaro. He led the brown mare slowly down the slope and into the valley, moving the horses at no more than a fast walk. The sun had slipped behind the distant hills when he reached the campground. Nora Thompson saw him and came running with a blanket. Ruth Simmons halted cleaning a dress as she saw him ride in, ducked into her lean-to, and reappeared with a bucket of water.

Fargo swung from the pinto and let the women bring Bess down and wrap her in the blanket. Most of the others gathered as the women took Bess into the Simmons' lean-to, and he told them what had happened.

"Damn them, we've got to hit back, somehow," Ollie Joust said, and the murmur of agreement rippled through the others.

Fargo's glance swept over the stolid farmers, the women and youngsters, Charlie Burrows and Abby Weeden, Ted Fuller's nervous twitch and darting eyes. He kept his grim sigh inside himself. "Hard proof is your only answer," he said. "Bide your time for now." He saw them turn away with dissatisfied mutterings and he unsaddled as night fell and the cooking fires were lighted. He'd just finished a quick rubdown of the Ovaro when he saw Nell Owens beckon to him from beside a small fire off to the side.

"Join me, Fargo," she said. "Got more than enough for myself. Good beef made the Mexican way. I lived down Mexico for a few years." She ladled the meat and beans onto a tin plate, the odor of it too delicious to pass up, and he sat down beside her. In the firelight, Nell Owens' young face seemed even younger, and the top three buttons of her brown shirt were opened to let her heavy breasts spill outward, white, full-fleshed mounds that carried an unvarnished earthiness. The woman settled down beside him and he smelled the hard soap and faint muskiness of her intermingled in a very strong, female scent as earthy as her heavy breasts. "You heard I was the first they railroaded. I figure that gives me first call on getting my land back," Nell Owens said between mouthfuls.

He watched her eyes flick to him, dark with unstated words. "Meaning what, exactly?" Fargo remarked.

"Meaning you see to proving how Lansing and the others stole my land, and you can have anything you want whenever you want it," the woman said. "Don't let the touch of gray in my hair fool you, Fargo."

"Wouldn't think of it," he said.

"I know how much woman I am," she said.

"Plenty, I'm sure," he said, and she caught the wryness in his smile.

"Somebody else come to you already?" Nell Owens asked.

"Same tune, different words," he answered. "I'll give you the same answer. Everybody put in to pay me.

Nobody gets special favors." He handed the emptied plate back to her. "Thanks for supper," he said.

Nell Owens half-smiled back and her wide-cheek-boned face held a simmering, throbbing sensuousness as she drew a deep breath and the heavy breasts rose in a fleshy wave. "Think on it, Fargo," she said as he rose, nodded, and retrieved his bedroll. He walked past the edge of the campground as the fires were extinguished, and climbed up a rise to a small clearing edged by thick red cedars.

Nell Owens stayed in his thoughts as he spread out his bedroll and undressed to his shorts in the warm night. She'd been the second to come trying to make a deal. Like Ted Fuller, it left a sour taste in his mouth and made him wonder about the others. Were they all really out for themselves, willing to undercut each other, only some without the boldness to admit it? Perhaps he was being unfair, he reflected. Maybe only a few were out only for themselves. He pushed aside the thoughts. It was too early for judgments.

He stretched, let the warm night wind blow across the powerful magnificence of his near-naked body. His eyes were half-closed when he caught the faint sound of foot-steps, quiet but not stealthy, and he listened. The foot-steps halted, moved on again, uncertain steps.

"Fargo?" he heard the call through the darkness, a woman's voice.

"Over here," he called softly, and watched the figure come into view, take on features as it drew near and the moon cast its pale light. He saw brown hair piled atop her head, hands clasped in front of her, a full-length dark-gray nightdress that helped cloak her in subdued subservience. "What're you doing here?" Fargo asked in surprise.

Mary Fuller's quiet shyness remained, but he saw her

eyes move over his body with a quick, flicking glance that returned to linger. "Ted sent me," she said very quietly.

He rose onto one elbow to frown at Mary Fuller. She was not unattractive, he realized again, only the subdued, held-in air making her seem mousy.

"Another try?" Fargo said. "You, instead of money?"

Mary Fuller dropped to her knees, and he saw her hands digging into each other. She nodded, her eyes fastened on the ground, and Fargo felt more than irritation at Ted Fuller's bald-faced play.

"Your brother's a real bastard," Fargo growled. Her held-in little face didn't change expression and her eyes stayed on the ground. "And you just go along with whatever he says to do." Mary Fuller nodded again, but this time she raised her eyes to meet his frown. "Why?" he barked.

She shrugged. "It's always been that way," she halfwhispered. "Always. The way we were raised, the way it turned out. I never knew any other way."

He felt a stab of pity for her through his anger. "Your problem, honey," he growled. "But you tell your brother he's lost out twice now. Tell him not to try for three."

Mary Fuller didn't move. "Don't just send me back," she murmured.

"Maybe you didn't understand. I'm not taking his offer. Don't take it personal, honey, but he's not buying me," Fargo said.

"I understand," Mary Fuller said, her voice growing stronger. "I understand, and I don't want you to send me back."

Fargo peered at her and saw tiny pinpoints of light in her eyes. "You want him to think I've taken him up on it?" He frowned. "No dice, honey."

"No. I'll tell him you turned down his offer," Mary Fuller said softly.

He peered at her and saw the subdued, held-in quality

had vanished from her face, her eyes dark and seething with sudden turmoil. "I'll be damned," Fargo breathed. "He sent you, but you came here for your own reasons."

The flash of spirit in Mary Fuller's face took him by surprise. "Yes, dammit," she snapped. "He's always ordering me to do this or that, and I never get anything out of it. This time he won't and I will." She reached up and pulled the tie at the neck of the nightdress to let it fall open. "I'd never have come here on my own, but he sent me and I'm here and I mightn't ever have another chance again," she said.

"The chance or the courage?" Fargo asked.

She paused a moment. "Either one," she answered, and her hands lifted, pulled the nightgown from her with one motion as she remained on her knees. Mary Fuller's naked body straightened for him and he saw good, broad shoulders, smooth firm skin, breasts that were not exciting yet not unattractive, long sloping tops that grew into moderately full undersides with small pink areolae surrounding equally small and pink nipples. Not unlike her face, Mary Fuller had an understated body, legs curving nicely enough, slightly rounded little belly, a modest triangle of tangled curliness—everything in order yet without excitement. Too many years of holding herself in, he thought as he reached out, closed one hand around her waist, and drew her to him. He saw the moment of fright cross her face and then she shook it away and buried her mouth against his shoulder.

His hands found the long topline of her breasts and traced a path down to the little pink nipples. Mary Fuller gasped, shuddered, and her arms encircled him with an almost desperate grip. He shed shorts and his burgeoning maleness fell against her. "Oh . . . oh, good God, good God," she half-sobbed, and drew her legs up. He waited until she slowly pulled her thighs back down, and he rolled to press half atop her. "Don't send me back," he heard her breathe in his ear. "Make love to me. Good God, Fargo, please make love to me." He heard the whisper grow into a sudden desperation and her arms tightened around him again. She arched her body backward and the longish breasts pushed up. He first pulled on one, then the other, drawing each into the warmth of his mouth. Mary Fuller lay almost motionless, her eyes wide open, unseeing, as he caressed her breasts, ran his hand down her abdomen and across her modest tangle of pubic hair. She lay still but made no protest as he pushed her thighs apart gently and explored the small, tight darkness of her sex.

"Ah . . . ah . . . ah . . . oh, good God," he heard her whisper and he probed, pressed, and felt her belly contract with an instant of pleasure-pain. "Do it, do it, please, please do it," Mary Fuller gasped out, and he caught the fear in her voice.

"Yes, relax, honey . . . relax," he said, but he knew the words meant nothing to her. He stroked, caressed, and she gave tiny groans, but her body continued to lie almost motionless and he felt a sudden urge to be done with it. He came over her, slid slowly into her, his throbbing organ almost too large to fit. Mary Fuller's eyes continued to stare up into nothingness, but he felt her knees draw up and she shuddered and cried out as he pushed in deeper. He began to move inside her, slowly, smoothly, and her gasps came with tiny moaning sounds that were sounds of pleasure, and yet she lay almost supinely under him. Only the tiny gasps evidenced that she felt, enjoyed, wanted, and he increased his tempo. The little sounds grew stronger and he felt her body tensing, tightening, and he began to thrust hard into her. Mary Fuller's mouth lay open, her lips parted, and she stared into the sky as her body continued to stay motionless until her legs suddenly lifted, pressing hard into his ribs.

"God, oh, my God," Mary Fuller suddenly screamed, a full-throated cry, and he felt her tighten around him as he exploded inside her. She screamed again, no words this time, only a long wail muffled against his shoulder as her pelvis made little shuddering motions, almost as though it were not attached to the rest of her body. He stayed in her, filling her completely, as she grew limp, her legs falling away from his ribs, her arms sliding from around him. He watched her head fall backward, eyes closed and lips parted, her breathing shallow and fast. He slowly drew away and lay beside her. He watched her eyes open and find his face. A smile touched her lips. She pushed herself onto one elbow and peered at him.

"Nothing to you, everything to me," she said simply.

"Don't knock yourself," he said.

"You don't have to be kind to me," she answered.

"All right, no kindness," he agreed. "You've been locked in so long it'll take time to come around."

"Think I can?" Mary Fuller asked.

"Sure you can, if you don't go back to your old ways, holding yourself in, living in his shadow," Fargo told her.

Her little smile surprised him again, full of suddenly very womanly wisdom. "I can't change me all of a sudden. But it won't ever be the same again," Mary Fuller said.

"He's still a bastard," Fargo growled.

She made no reply as she pulled the nightdress on and the smug little smile was still on her lips as she left without another word.

When she disappeared from sight, Fargo lay back on his bedroll. Mary Fuller had become more than a woman tonight. She'd taken the first step to becoming a person, and he felt good about that. It was the only thing he felt good about, he reminded himself. The job had turned into a morass of questions, too many things that didn't make sense. Nothing fitted the pattern he had expected. It was time to make things happen, and he fell asleep holding the thought, his plans already formed.

When morning came, he waited for the camp to wake before saddling up. He saw Abby Weeden helping Charlie with an overflowing basket of laundry. As he led the Ovaro past the Thompsons' lean-to, Ruth stepped out, and he paused as she met his glance.

"She still hurts pretty bad, but you can see her," the woman said.

Fargo nodded and stepped inside the hut. Bess looked up at him from under a white sheet. She blinked and let herself look chastened. "I'm sorry," she murmured.

"Sorry isn't enough. You're a damn pain in the ass." He scowled. "First, you talk me into this thing, and then you make yourself the biggest problem."

"I'll make it up to you," she said.

"By doing what I tell you to do," he said sternly. "I won't go saving your neck again."

"You won't have to," Bess said meekly, and he turned and strode from the hut. "Promise," he heard her call after him as he swung onto his horse. He rode from the campground and made his way down the middle of the valley, across land that now waited for Dorrance Lansing to take over. Put together, it made up most of the center of the valley and a good part of the lower slopes on both sides. Why this land? The question kept arising. It was good, lush land, but no better and no more fertile than the land on either side of the valley that lay there just for the taking. Greed wasn't reason enough. There had to be something more.

He was still pondering the questions when he left the valley and rode on to Lansing's ranch. He saw three figures outside the ranch house as he neared. Blond hair glinting in the sunlight marked Dorrance Lansing as one. As he drew closer, he saw the other two were Sheriff Curry and Judge Tolliver. Both men turned harsh eyes on him as he rode to a halt. "Well, now, just who we came looking for," the sheriff said.

"You always come here when you want to find somebody?" Fargo asked mildly.

"I figured you were working for Mr. Lansing and he might have a lead on you," the sheriff said. Fargo saw the man draw his breath in and straighten his square figure. "I've had all I'm going to take from you, Fargo. You're not shooting up any more of my deputies doing their job."

"Their job beating a girl half to death?" Fargo asked, his voice even.

"They weren't doing that," the sheriff snapped.

"That bastard without a nose tell you that?" Fargo said.

"No, he's barely alive. Dave Holloway told me when he brought Strainer in."

"He's lying and covering up. Or maybe you gave the orders in the first place," Fargo returned.

"I just told them to bring the girl in," the sheriff said.

Judge Tolliver broke in. "No matter, I've a warrant here for your arrest for interferin' with lawful deputies doing their job," he said, and pulled the warrant from his pocket.

"Hold that up so's I can see it," Fargo said, and the judge held his court order out at arm's length. Fargo's hand drew the Colt in a smooth motion too fast to follow, and he fired a single shot. The warrant disintegrated as Judge Tolliver's gaunt face stared at his hand with a mixture of astonishment, awe, and fright. "I don't see any warrant," Fargo said quietly. He saw Judge Tolliver's gaunt face grow ashen and the man pulled at the sheriff's arm.

"Let's go, Roy," Tolliver breathed.

Fargo saw the sheriff's small features seemed to have

gathered into a knot in the center of his square head as he glared back. "I don't like this, Fargo, none of it," the sheriff growled.

"I'm real upset about that," Fargo said as he holstered the Colt.

"Another time, another place," the sheriff said.

"Whenever," Fargo answered, and watched the man climb onto his horse, the judge's spindly frame mounting his own animal with anxious haste. The two men rode away and Fargo felt Dorrance Lansing's eyes on him. He dismounted and met the man's glance.

"The sheriff is just trying to do his job," Lansing said.

"You keep saying that," Fargo replied.

"It seems you're making a habit of rescuing that Hanford girl," Lansing commented as he led the way into the house.

"Seems that way," Fargo agreed. "That bother you?"

"No, so long as it doesn't interfere with what you're doing for me," Dorrance Lansing said, and Fargo's eyes studied the man's face but saw only mild blandness. Once again, he found none of the cold strength he expected to see in Lansing, and the absence of it bothered him. The man didn't seem to fit the clever ruthlessness of events. He decided to be sharp and fastened Dorrance Lansing with a hard glance.

"I don't like it when people don't level with me," he said, and drew a quick frown from the man. "Why didn't you tell me you hired others to find the silver?" he tossed out, and saw Lansing swallow and redden.

"I didn't think it was important," Lansing said.

"Everything's important," Fargo barked.

"They didn't find anything," Lansing said, and seemed apologetic.

"How do you know they didn't find anything? Maybe one of them did and took off with it," Fargo suggested.

Lansing looked uncomfortable. "No," he said. "Their

bodies were both found at the bottom of Black Canyon, washed out by the river. They must have fallen."

Fargo nodded as he rejected the answer. Both men falling was too much of a coincidence. Lansing was holding something back. "The place was easy enough to find with the map. Why didn't you go after it yourself?" Fargo questioned.

"I told you, I'm no good at that sort of thing," Dorrance Lansing said. "That's why I hired those other two. I wanted a professional. But they weren't in your class."

Fargo nodded and was more certain the man wasn't leveling with him. "I'm going to start digging tonight," he said casually.

"Tonight? Excellent," Lansing said, and his excitement seemed genuine.

"Just wanted you to know," Fargo said as he started from the house.

Lansing hurried along beside him and almost bubbled with excitement. "You'll tell me if you find anything," he said. "I don't care how late it is. My men have been told you can come and go as you please."

"If I find anything," Fargo said as he mounted the Ovaro. Dorrance Lansing waved to him as he rode away, and Fargo let the frown inside himself slide over his brow. Dorrance Lansing was holding something back. That was plain enough. He was playing his own game, whatever it was. But he still didn't show the kind of pure greed or ruthless strength that ought to be a part of him.

But the bait had been tossed out, Fargo grunted silently. There was plenty of time for Lansing to get word to the sheriff before nightfall. He sent the Ovaro into a trot as he entered the valley and headed back to the camp. He'd have at least one answer before the night was over, he told himself.

6

He rode into the first twisting rock passage of Black Canyon before the moon had crested the peaks. Hanging far back, four horsemen followed him. The kerosene lamp he held on the saddle in front of him was turned low, but the glow was more than enough for the four riders to see. He'd chosen the four, though there'd been plenty of instant volunteers back at the camp—Tad and Kelby Joust, Fred Thompson, and Ned Simmons. He'd outlined his plan in brief and paused at Thea's tent as she watched from the entranceway.

"Get everything done in Saddle Rock?" he asked.

"Yes." She nodded. "And hurried like hell to get back."

"Sorry." He smiled.

"Stop by when you get back," Thea said.

"Could be real late," he told her.

"I'll be here," she said, and he'd ridden from the camp then while the night was still new, the others hanging back just in case there were eyes watching. But he didn't expect that. He expected they'd wait, give him plenty of time to make the slow trip high into the canyon and begin to dig. The kerosene lamp would be a beacon for them, pinpointing his presence.

The twisting passages through the canyon took more time by night and he rode with the map held open under the base of the lamp. The moon had moved high into the blue-velvet sky when he finally reached the circular area, and he dismounted, set the lamp down alongside the spiral of red clay, and waited for the others to arrive. When they finally rode into the circle of stone, he pointed to the narrow passageways that ran through the rocks around them.

"Each man takes one for himself. You stay in there out of sight," Fargo said. "You'll hear them when they reach here. When you do, come out shooting."

"We've got it," Tad Joust said. He rode his horse into the nearest narrow pass through the tall rocks, and Fargo watched as the others picked a passage and moved into it until he was alone again in the circle of stone. He pulled the pick and shovel that Fred Thompson had supplied from the back of his saddle and decided to use the pick, first, over the area where the others had dug. He swung the pick hard and felt it dig into the red clay. Using a crisscross pattern, he worked steadily, paused only when arms and back insisted on relief. Alternating pick and shovel, he dug out a fair-sized portion of the hard red clay and found only more clay. He finally halted when the moon began to slide down the far side of the towering rock formations. He slid down against a wall of black rock and let an angry sigh escape him.

The bait had gone untouched. He'd set up what seemed a perfect chance to get rid of him and they'd let it go by. That didn't fit, either. The sheriff wasn't the kind to miss an opportunity. Fargo cursed softly as a surge of emotions raced through him—disappointment, chagrin, wonderment. He pushed himself to his feet and lifted the lamp to survey his diggings. He'd chopped away a good piece of the red clay, but he saw only more clay beneath and he turned away. He turned the lamp off as he called to the others and watched as they slowly emerged from the rock passageways.

"Something went wrong," Kelby Joust said.

"Maybe," Fargo said. "Or maybe I just have to figure out what this means." He left it at that, swung onto the Ovaro, and led the way down the precipitous canyon paths. The distant sound of the rushing river far below in the gorge echoed up through the silence of the night and the moon was almost out of sight at the horizon when they ended the long descent. He reached the still camp and halted as the others went on to their tents. Weary yet restless, he unsaddled his horse, took his bedroll, and paused at Thea's tent. He pulled the flap back, slipped silently inside, and saw her sit up at once, her sharp-pointed little breasts beautifully silhouetted against the tent as the dawn tinged the sky.

"I couldn't sleep," she said. "I'm been lying here awake." He slid down to his knees beside her and she reached out and began undoing his shirt buttons.

"They didn't bite," he told her.

"You're upset about that," Thea said.

"I keep wondering if I figured on something I shouldn't have," Fargo thought aloud.

"What's that mean?" Thea asked with a little frown as she pulled his shirt from him.

"I keep wondering about Dorrance Lansing," Fargo said. "Maybe he's not what everyone says he is."

"He's just more clever and more careful than you think," Thea answered.

"Maybe, but I don't read him that way," Fargo said.

"You ever read someone wrong?" she asked with an edge.

"It's happened," he admitted wryly. "Maybe he is a hell of a lot smarter than he seems."

Her fingers pulled at his gun belt and he helped her push his trousers away. Thea was atop him at once, her small, lithe body wrapped around him, legs rubbing up and down his thighs, hips lifting to touch his flat stomach, then moving downward again with twisting, serpentine motions. "Jesus, you're all I thought about since last time," she breathed as her hands reached for him, closed around him. "Oh, Christ . . . aaaaah . . . eeeee, oh, yes, yes," she gasped out as she stroked, caressed, rubbed her flat little belly against the throbbing warmth as her legs made almost frantic little motions. She pulled on him as she fell to the side and brought him over on top of her. Her legs came up at once to coil around his hips and she pushed her pubic mound upward, seeking, asking. "Now, Jesus, take me, Fargo, Fargo . . . Jesus," she cried out, and he let himself enter her. She half-screamed in pleasure. He half-swallowed one little breast, caressing it inside his mouth as Thea writhed and twisted with his every thrust. Her lithe, sinuous body seemed to coil and uncoil around him as her legs and arms moved up and down his body, and yet she moved with his thrusts, gasping out little cries with each sliding motion until he felt her flat little belly contract under him.

"Coming . . . oh, Jesus, I'm coming . . . Fargo, Fargo . . . come with me, oh, oh, ooooh," Thea cried out, and he hurried himself, managed to catch up to the frantic contractions seizing her as she erupted, screamed ecstasy into his chest. Once again, her legs never ceased their sliding, coiling, rubbing, uncoiling as she climaxed, and when the last screamed shudder passed through her and her fingers fell away from where they dug into his back, her legs continued their sinuous, slow rubbing. Finally, they, too, fell away and she lay half under him, green-gray eyes studying his face. "Some things go wrong, some go right," she murmured.

"Guess so." He laughed. "I'd better be on my way before the rest of the camp wakes up."

"Didn't think you'd be bothered about that," Thea said with an edge of sarcasm.

He paused pulling on clothes to look at her. "I'm not, but I thought you might be," he said.

She made a surprisingly harsh little sound. "I don't give a damn what they think or don't think," Thea said, and caught the moment in his eyes. "Surprised?" She laughed.

"Guess I shouldn't be," Fargo said. "For a group working together to get their lands back, everybody seems to be out for themselves. Here you go all the way to Saddle Rock to get supplies because you get the best deal and it's good for everybody, and yet you say you don't give a damn about the others."

"Dorrance Lansing and his sheriff and judge have thrown us together. That's where it starts and ends," Thea said, and her smile was unexpectedly warm. "Maybe I sounded too harsh. I've just never cared much about what other folks think." She rose, almost springing onto her feet in a quick, lithe motion, and pressed her small, naked litheness to him. "Get some sleep," she said.

"Just what I plan to do," he said. He left her, slipped from the tent, and hurried across the campground. Thea Manning was a little package of surprises, he reflected, steel under the small, lithe warmth of her. He carried his bedroll high up the slope until he found a little arbor of white birch shaded from the new sun. He lay down and slept, quickly and heavily.

The noon sun hung high in the sky when he woke and made his way back down to the camp. Everyday chores were being done as he brought his gear back to the Ovaro. Word about the night had gone through the camp. Ollie Joust expressed sympathy and Charlie Burrows came up with more of the same. "Goin' to try to smoke them out again?" he asked.

"Maybe," Fargo said as he sat down and started to unroll some beef jerky.

Mary Fuller appeared with a plate of hash. "Please," she said, and her smile was quick and warm.

"How are you doing?" he asked.

"Ted's still real mad at me," she said, her hands clasped demurely in front of her. "But I don't care," she added. He laughed. Mary Fuller was doing well.

"Thanks," he said as he returned the emptied plate to her.

She bent low, her voice a murmur. "You know the one thing I've been thinking about?" she asked.

"I can guess," he said.

"I'd be better the next time," she said.

"I'm sure of it," he told her.

She straightened, her eyes almost twinkling as she hurried away.

He wondered, not if Mary Fuller would come seeking him again, but only how long it would take her. He glanced up, saw Charlie Burrows watching him and Abby Weeden's trim, gray-haired figure approaching. She brushed past Charlie Burrows as though he weren't there.

"Got to ask you something, Fargo," the little old woman snapped. "You planning on leading this bunch against Dorrance Lansing and the sheriff's men?"

"Hell, no." Fargo frowned. "Where'd you get that idea?" Her sharp glance at Charlie was his answer.

"Now, hold on, Abby. I didn't exactly say that," Charlie said.

"You as much as said it, Charlie Burrows," Abby Weeden flung back hotly.

"Just what did you say, Charlie?" Fargo cut in.

"Only that it's likely it'll have to come to that," Charlie said.

"Hah! Roy Curry would like that, all right," Abby snapped. "Even with Fargo, here, leading you." Fargo heard his laugh at the little woman's peppery accuracy. Her eyes snapped to him. "Thanks for answering me. I didn't expect you'd be planning any such damn-fool move," she said.

"Not if I can help it," he agreed, and Abby Weeden strode away.

"That woman's prickly as a damn cactus," Charlie said.

"That woman's as smart as she's prickly," Fargo said. "The others think the way you do, that it'll come to that?"

"Most do," Charlie said. "They hope you'll come up with something else, but hope's running kind of low around here."

"Understandable," Fargo said as he saddled the Ovaro.

"Going off to see Lansing?" Charlie asked.

"Going to Black Canyon," Fargo said. "Want a better look at my diggings last night. If there really is silver there and I can find it, maybe we can use it to bargain with Lansing."

Charlie's lips pursed. "Never thought of that," he said. "Maybe you'll find something just as good. Somebody will, someday, up there."

"How's that?" Fargo questioned.

"Black Canyon, it's full of precious stones," the little man said. "Did a fair amount of prospecting in my day. I know rocks when I see them."

"Those black rocks valuable?" Fargo pressed.

"Those black rocks are what they call schists and they're where you find garnets, quartz, amethyst. I'd guess they'll find iron, manganese, nickel, potassium, and calcium in Black Canyon one day and you'll be seeing a big mining and hauling operation." The little man paused as he saw Fargo's frown as he peered hard at him.

"Go on," Fargo said.

"Of course, some folks will mine for precious stones such as garnet, but a lot more will go in for commercial beds such as the iron, nickel, and the potassium," Charlie speculated aloud.

"And the best route for any mining and hauling operations would be right through the valley. Any other way would take a lot more time and money," Fargo said, and felt the excitement pushing at him. "I think you just answered one question, Charlie. Anyone holding all the land through the center of the valley could make a nice dollar charging a fat right-of-passage fee."

Fargo watched Charlie's eyes darken as the impact of the words sank in. "By God," Charlie whispered. "*By God!*"

"That's why this land," Fargo said as he swung onto the Ovaro. "Now something fits for the first time." He wheeled the horse and sent it into a fast canter as he headed for the canyon. He rode with a feeling of elation. He had one answer, finally. Of course, there was still too much that didn't make sense. It didn't answer why Lansing and the sheriff were letting the valley people remain camped together, it didn't answer the transparency of Lansing's job offer, and it didn't explain away the lack of cold strength in Lansing. Nor did it explain why no one had taken the bait the night before. But maybe one answer would be a beginning and he hurried the pinto on to the canyon.

He drew the map from his pocket and studied it again as he climbed the twisting rock passages and carefully rode the narrow ledge beside the gorge. He was certain he'd made no mistakes when he reached the high rock circle and dismounted. Map in hand, he swept the area with his eyes and came to rest on the red clay he had dug during the night. Unless the map was marked wrongly, it was the spot. But he had seen hand-drawn maps before that were marked wrong. He walked the perimeter of the uneven circle and paused before each of the black and gray-white granite areas to search the ground, the openings of the passageways into the rock formations. He paused to wipe his brow as the sun burned hard and he felt the perspiration coating his back and shoulders. The map had to be marked correctly, the spiral of red clay the only area where anything could have been hidden, and he turned again to his diggings.

Squatting down, he wiped his forehead again as he poked through the hard pieces of broken clay. He had dug plenty deep, he saw, deeper than he'd realized, deep enough to have come upon anything buried there. A man wouldn't bury a cache so far down it'd take days to unearth it.

Fargo rested himself on one knee and wiped the back of his neck with his kerchief as the sun blazed down. He let thoughts revolve. According to Lansing, the silver had been buried years and years ago. Simple wind and soil erosion should have brought it closer to the surface, if anything. Maybe there never was any buried silver, despite what Lansing thought, he mused. He'd just shaken a bead of perspiration from his forehead and he stared at the diggings when it happened, a shadow, first, against the gray-white granite to his right. Only a shadow, and he cursed softly as he slowly turned, one hand on the Colt at his hip.

He stared up at the arrow poised on a drawn bowstring and, behind it, the bare-chested figure on the spotted pony. He let his eyes shift to the right and take in the five other figures at the edge of the rocks, each with an arrow aimed at him. Only a shadow, he cursed inwardly, not a sound as they'd come through the narrow rock passages silent as ghosts. Ute, he grunted to himself as he saw the pattern on the nearest Indian's moccasins. Slowly, he took his hand from the holster and rose to his feet.

The nearest Indian wore two armbands with beaded design work, and Fargo saw the man had his bear-greased hair pulled back into a knot at the back of his head. The Indian bore a slash of a scar on one shoulder and Fargo saw two of the others slide from their mounts and hurry to him. They pulled the Colt from its holster and the others lowered their drawn bowstrings. The Ute with the scarred shoulder seemed to be the leader of the party, and there was no mistaking the cold hate in his eyes.

The Ute spoke the Shoshonean tongue, one Fargo understood well enough, but even if he hadn't, there was little to misunderstand in the Indian's manner. The man raised his arm, pointed his finger at the tall man in front of him. "You die," he said. "Black Canyon belong to the Ute. Only the Ute can come here. You die."

Fargo, unmoving, saw two other braves rush up to pin his arms behind him, and he felt the rawhide thongs bind his wrists together. The Ute with the scarred shoulder motioned and Fargo felt the sharp prod in his back as one of the others pushed him forward with the tip of his bow. The top brave turned his pony into one of the narrow passages and Fargo followed, the others filing in behind him. The passage led upward, and when he reached the top, his shirt was soaked with perspiration. He stepped onto a flat rock ledge that bordered the deep chasm, the Gunnison River far below.

As he watched, two more of the Utes dismounted and came forward with a long piece of lariat. They stretched it the length of the ledge and secured both ends into crevices and wrapped them around slivers of stone. The lariat stretched approximately waist high, he noted. He watched as the two Indians took another, shorter piece of lariat, tied it around his neck, and with a loose knot, secured it to the taut length of rope.

Fargo, frowned, wondered what they were arranging, and then one jabbed him in the ribs with a short-handled lance. He moved along the taut length of rope. Another jab sent him moving again. A third jab from the other side sent him moving in the other direction along the taut length of rope. They were showing him he could move back and forth along the entire length of the taut rope, and he saw the Ute with the scarred shoulder glance up at the sun. Suddenly Fargo's frown turned into a silent curse.

They were not simply going to leave him to die under the searing rays of the sun. They were going to extract the last measure of cruelty from it. The rope around his neck was long enough so that he could lie on the ground, or go back and forth on the taut length of lariat. The burning sun would dry a man up in hours. The scorching rays would sear into his body and his brain to drive him into a frenzy to escape its rays. He would rush the length of the rope to try to find some relief, some shelter from the inescapable, pitiless rays. Only there would be no shelter and he would use up what little strength was left inside him. He would go mad from the searing rays and from his inability to find shelter, the twisting frustration far worse than if he'd been staked down in one place.

Fargo glanced at the Utes and cursed their diabolic cruelty. The scarred shoulder dismounted and lifted his arms to the burning sun. He chanted his words as the others murmured in echo.

"Great Sun God of the Ute, this intruder is yours. Destroy him. Turn him into dry dust. Draw the living fluids from him and leave him a shell. When you are through with him, we shall throw him down to the River God below."

Fargo let a harsh sound escape his lips. He had just

learned why the other two men Lansing had hired were found at the bottom of the gorge. He watched as the Ute turned away from his chanting and pulled himself onto his pony. He headed upward through a narrow pass and the others followed.

Fargo lost sight of the Indians for a few minutes and then saw them reappear atop a higher ledge. The Ute leader halted there and looked down at him. As Fargo watched, the Utes moved their horses into the shade of the tall crags, each settling himself to look down at their victim below. Fargo cursed grimly. They would stay there and watch his every move. They would watch and wait for the sun to do everything the Ute leader had asked of it.

"Bastards," he half-shouted. "Lousy, stinking bastards."

The Utes sat motionless on their ponies pressed against the shadows of the tall crags.

"Goddamn bastards," he called again. They'd wait and enjoy their spectacle of hellish cruelty. If he were not driven mad or baked to death by dark, they would simply wait through the night and watch the morning sun finish the job. The double-edged throwing knife was in its calf holster around his leg, but he didn't dare try to reach it under their unwavering eyes. He had to somehow hold out till dark, somehow keep from being driven mad till then. He swore at the Utes again, under his breath this time.

Slowly, he gathered himself, pulled in every fiber of his entire being. He'd use anger as a weapon, but not the wild fury that would only help burn himself up from the inside. He'd use cold, controlled rage, the hate that would give him disciplined strength to draw upon. Even as he gathered himself, he felt the power of the sun burning into him as if in answer to his defiance.

The rope around his neck was long enough to let him

reach the ground, and he lowered himself to sit cross-legged. He closed his eyes and drew upon all he had learned over the years—the wisdom of the wild, the discipline of the hunter, the inner power that fed outer strength, the knowledge of man, and the instincts of nature. He'd need all of it, he knew as he sat motionless. He felt the burning rays drying his body, reaching through his skin, pulling energy and body fluids from him. He felt as though he were being pressed down by a giant, invisible hand, and it wasn't long before the waves of weakness began to sweep over him. His hat afforded some protection but not enough, and the weight of it suddenly became unbearable. It constricted him, seemed to tighten around his head, and he resisted the urge to pull it from him. Dizziness swept through him, and he pulled his dried lips back and summoned hate to fight away the light-headedness. He kept himself motionless, refused to fall on his side, braced by the crossed position of his legs, and the sun burned with its unceasing, scorching power. His thoughts wavered, drifted away into nothing, and slowly returned, wavered, alternated between flashes of biting clarity and fuzzy indistinction.

The pitiless sun blazed, almost as if it were actually responding to the Indian's chant, and Fargo felt actual physical pain, his skin burning, his throat raw and parched, and it seemed almost as if his bones were drying out. He felt the tremendous urge to pull himself up and try to find shelter, some spot of shade or a place where the wind came around a crag. It took every ounce of his self-discipline to fight the urge. They watched, he told himself, cursing their satanic ways. They watched, but they were not dealing with an ordinary man, he swore silently. He'd beat them yet, he told himself, letting cold rage fill his dried, parched body. The bastards, he cursed again.

Time vanished. The canyon became a blur, then a void, and there was nothingness. Except for the searing, burning sun, the consuming, shriveling rays. Again, he fought away the urge to move, to find some shelter the way a blind mole scurries to find a hole. "Bastards," he muttered through a throat that allowed him only to whisper. "Bastards."

But he stayed unmoving, husbanding every last ounce of strength inside him, sheer willpower and inner drive keeping him conscious and alive. At moments he wondered if he really were alive. He seemed weightless, completely dried away, suspended in some netherworld. He kept his eyes closed, aware he still lived only when a flashing moment of pain coursed through him. It was his skin that first told him something had changed, a prickly sensation, the terrible burning gone. Slowly, he pulled his dried eyelids open and felt the pain of it. He managed to blink and focus; he first saw only the void, and then the void took on dark craggy shapes and he lifted his head and felt the pain of blistered skin at the back of his neck. He stared up at the night sky and felt softness against his skin as a warm wind puffed fitfully.

He heard the silent laughter as it welled up inside him. He had made the night. He had won the first part of the fight. The knowledge sent a renewed surge of strength through him, and slowly, painfully, he pushed himself onto his knees, stayed there as circulation finally returned to the rest of his legs. Grimacing with pain, he pushed himself onto his feet, swayed, and fought off the wave of dizziness that swept over him. The night was moonless and he stood in a black circle, the rope around his neck reminding him of the rest of his task. The Utes were up there, he knew. They were asleep now, confident they had only to wait for the morning sun. Bastards, he growled silently as he fell to his knees.

He groped behind himself with his bound wrists, sank

down until he could reach the end of his trousers and pull the trouser leg up enough for his fingers to close around the hilt of the knife in the calf holster. Carefully, keeping a firm grip on the weapon, he drew it free of its holster and sank back onto his legs, thoroughly exhausted from the effort. He waited till enough strength flowed back into his dried-out body, and swallowing in pain, he turned the double-edged knife in his hands until he could begin to saw against the rawhide thongs. He could only make tiny little movements and he had to rest every few minutes as his hands cramped. The rawhide thongs were new and tough, and he cursed at the tiny cut he'd made after what seemed hours.

He changed position often to rest his legs, and he felt the dehydrated weakness of his body. Each little sawing motion was an effort and he knew the night was moving inexorably to the dawn, and the rawhide thongs still held. He renewed his efforts, drew on renewed strength, short-lived as it was, and continued to saw at the wrist bonds until finally he felt the cut had grown deep, almost through the rawhide. He pulled his wrists apart and cursed. Normally he'd have been able to snap the thongs with the power of his arm and shoulder muscles. But now he had only dried and seared muscles, a body without strength, acting on determination and the universal will to survive.

He returned to sawing at the thongs, and when he suddenly felt them part, he toppled onto his back and lay still for a long moment. He brought his wrists around in front of him, pulled the rest of the thongs free with his teeth, and began to rub circulation back into his wrists. He finally pulled himself to his knees and his eyes widened in horror. A faint pink streak moved across the sky, dawn sending its first tentative fingers to push away the night.

The Utes would be awake too soon. The ledge where

he waited was still in blackness but the first dawn light would be there in hardly any time at all. Fargo rose to his feet, cut the lariat from around his neck with the knife, and stepped free. He felt the weakness of his body. He could never battle even one Ute, to say nothing of six. He had to be ready for them with a weapon, and that meant getting to his horse with the big Sharps rifle in the saddle holster.

He moved forward, swayed, shook his head, and pulled himself on again. The rock pass wasn't too steep, but it felt as though he were climbing the tallest mountain in the world. He slid to the ground often, only to force himself on again. He saw the sky growing light and cursed silently. Had he survived, had he fought off the merciless sun only to lose anyway? He shook away the thought, and his lips drew back in anger as he half-crawled the last few feet of the pass to the higher ledge where the Utes had positioned themselves.

He lay on his stomach and peered into the area of flat rock. They were still asleep, each man beside his horse, and he saw the Ovaro to his right—nearby, yet so far away. He began to crawl forward, inching his way along the stone and fighting off the waves of exhaustion that swept over him. He heard one of the Indians stir, turn, make a noise with his mouth, and the pink-gray light was stronger now, beginning to flood the sky. He crawled forward again, hurrying; he reached the Ovaro and rose to his knees. He rested one hand against the gleaming white midsection of the horse as he pulled the rifle from its holster. Turning, he crawled back to the pass, the big Sharps in his hand. He'd just reached the front of the pass when he heard the Indians come awake. He half-slid down the passage, halted halfway down, and turned where the pass made a small curve. Staying on his stomach, he brought the rifle to his shoulder, took aim, and waited.

It took but a moment when he heard the shouts, recognized the voice of the Ute with the scarred shoulder. They had looked down to the ledge below and, with disbelief, seen that their victim was gone. He heard the sound of them as they flung themselves onto their ponies and the sharp clatter of horses' hooves resounded down the narrow passageway. Two rounded the little curve first, two more close behind them. Fargo fired from his prone position and the first two Indians toppled from their ponies. The second two tried to rein to a halt, but Fargo fired again, the sound of the big Sharps cannonlike in the narrow passage. The second two Utes fell against each other as they toppled, one with his chest blown apart, the other almost without his head.

Fargo heard the shout, the scarred-shoulder Ute bringing his pony to a halt. Fargo slid backward, down the pass, reloading as he did. He stayed flat on his stomach, the rifle ready to fire again, his eyes fixed on the narrow curve of the pass. He guessed the Ute had backtracked to get up more speed. He'd come racing down the passage, the other one behind him, leap over his fallen comrades, and trust to speed to rush his foe.

Fargo braced himself, stopped the trembling that coursed through one arm. He waited and heard only silence. Nothing moved at the curve in the little passage, and he frowned, blinked, and suddenly felt the curse inside himself as he threw himself onto his back. The Ute's figure rose at the edge of the rock side of the passage, on foot, his arm drawn back to fire an arrow.

Fargo saw the Ute release the bowstring and he fired the big Sharps, two shots. He flung himself to one side, but he had time to see the Ute clutch his abdomen, sink to his knees, and begin to topple from the crag. Fargo heard the arrowhead slam into the stone a fraction of an inch from the back of his neck as he kept rolling, came up against the other side of the passage, the rifle ready to fire again. He heard the dull, thudding sound of the Ute's body landing somewhere below him on the rocks and then, moments later, the sharp sound of a horse racing away up through the canyon passages.

He lay quietly and listened to the harsh, wheezing sound of his own breathing until he regained enough strength to push himself to his feet. Climbing over the grotesque, still forms of the four Utes, he spotted his Colt tied to the waistband of one, and he retrieved the gun. He pulled himself up again to where the Ovaro waited at the top of the passage. He fell upon his canteen, hands trembling as he opened the spout, but he forced himself to take little sips until his dried and knotted stomach could absorb more of the liquid. Finally he slid to the ground and slowly finished emptying the canteen. He lay flat on his back for a spell before rising and clambering into the saddle. Letting the horse make its own way down the canyon, he clung to the saddle horn as the Ovaro negotiated the narrow ledge alongside the gorge.

When he reached the bottom of the canyon, the green grass seemed an oasis. He halted at the first stream, tore his shirt off, and lay in the rushing water. He turned over, let the cool, clear water lap against his body until he finally began to feel less like a piece of dust. He rested beside the stream to let his strength slowly return, and finally mounted the Ovaro again—far from his normal self, yet strong enough to pay Lansing a visit. The campground lay in his path, though, and he decided to pause no longer than necessary as the afternoon began to wane.

Fred Thompson was first to see him ride in and hurried toward him as others quickly gathered. "Where've you been?" the man asked, and peered at him. "You don't look so good."

Fargo saw Nell Owens appear, staring at him. Charlie Burrows speared him with his sharp eyes.

"Six Utes decided to turn me into a fried egg," Fargo said. "But I'm here, and that's all that counts. I'll be back later." He saw Thea come to the flap of her tent as he rode off, her eyes following him with concern. But he rode on and made his way down the center of the valley until he reached the other end and turned toward Dorrance Lansing's place. He'd decided to really push Lansing this time, enough to make the man drop any mask he might be wearing. It wouldn't be difficult, Fargo murmured, his anger more than eager to erupt.

The night had begun to move over the land when he reached the spread. The bunkhouse was brightly lit as was the stable, and Dorrance Lansing opened the door of the ranch house as Fargo dismounted. "I thought I'd hear from you before this," Lansing said accusingly. "I told you I'd be waiting."

Fargo strode past him into the house and Lansing closed the door. "So you did," he growled.

"Did you find anything?" the man asked with irritable impatience.

"Yes," Fargo said, and watched excitement flood Dorrance Lansing's face. The man opened his mouth to ask further questions when Fargo's hands shot out as though they were pistons. He seized Lansing and lifted the man from the floor. "Utes, six of them, damn near killed me," Fargo roared, and shook Lansing as though he were a rag doll. "You knew the Utes look on Black Canyon as theirs. That's why you never went up after the silver yourself. You were too damn afraid."

"Please, Fargo—listen to me," Lansing stammered.

"Go to hell," Fargo said, and flung Lansing halfway across the room where he crashed into one of the heavy chairs and fell sprawling onto the floor. "You didn't tell the other two you hired, either, and they're dead because of it. I ought to break your goddamn neck." He took a threatening step forward and watched to see if the man reacted with any steel. But Dorrance Lansing showed only fear in his face as he scooted backward, crablike, across the floor.

"No, wait. Listen to me, Fargo," he pleaded. "You're right—I knew, and I was afraid to go myself. I didn't tell you because I was afraid you wouldn't go then, either." He pushed himself to his feet and blinked away some of the fear in his eyes. "Did you find anything else?" he asked.

Fargo chose words, his answer prepared. "Enough," he said carefully.

Dorrance Lansing's eyes widened at once. "What does that mean?" he asked.

"Enough to make me think it might be there," Fargo said.

"Then you'll go back, you'll keep on?" Lansing said eagerly.

"I didn't say that," Fargo answered.

"I'll double the money up front," Lansing said.

Fargo let himself consider the offer. "All right," he said after a long pause. "Next time I go back, I'll be on guard. I'll be watching for them." The words were not an untruth and Fargo saw Lansing rush to the desk, unlock a drawer, and pull out another roll of bills. He pushed it at Fargo and the big man took the money with his stern face unchanged, his eyes peering sharply at Dorrance Lansing's eager, half-apologetic face. "I'll be in touch," he said as he turned on his heel and strode from the house. He swung onto the Ovaro and rode into the darkness, Lansing watching from the doorway.

Fargo let his thoughts sort themselves out as he rode through the valley. Once again, he had answers that were not really answers. But something was very wrong. Dorrance Lansing had shown only selfish weakness, even cowardice. He'd shown no strength at all. The man just wasn't what he was painted as being, unless he was the world's best goddamn actor. By the time he reached the camp he'd decided to nail down his thoughts further. The camp had already bedded down. He halted the Ovaro outside Thea's tent and left the saddle on the horse.

Thea greeted him as he reached the tent flap and he stepped inside as her green-gray eyes studied him. "What happened?" she asked and he told her quickly.

"He doesn't fit. Something's all wrong," he told her as he finished.

"Such as?" she asked, her eyes narrowed at him.

"Don't know, but something." He grimaced.

"I say you're wrong about Dorrance," Thea answered.

"I saw him fall apart," Fargo snapped. "No steel in him at all."

"A rat isn't going to take on a wolf. That doesn't make him less a rat," Thea answered, and the truth of her words made him pause and grimace again.

"True enough," he conceded. "But I'm going to get into his place. I want to look through that desk where he keeps his papers."

"Why?" she questioned.

"Legal's been so important to them it's got to mean claims. But he hasn't moved to take over any land. If he hasn't filed the claims yet, they'll be there. If he has, he'll have copies. I want to see them for myself," Fargo said.

Thea shrugged. "It's stupid. You could risk your neck, tip your hand, and find nothing," she said.

"That's why I came to see you." Fargo grinned. "You know any way in except through the front door or a window?"

Her eyes narrowed at him. "You think he sneaked me in and out when he was chasing me?" she stabbed.

"Likely as not," he answered. "You had a jealous man then."

Thea's smile was slow. "There's a storm-cellar door in the back of the house. You go down and take the first steps. It comes up at the back of the living room," she said.

"Thanks," Fargo said as she slid her arms around his neck.

"I was worried about you last night when you didn't come back," she murmured.

"So was I," he grunted.

Her arms tightened and her lips found his mouth, and he felt the points of her little breasts push into his chest. "Stay, forget your wild-goose chase," she said.

"Can't," he said as he pulled back. Her little smile stayed, became edged with something close to cynicism as he backed out of the tent. He took the Ovaro's reins and walked the horse across the sleeping camp. He had just reached the Thompsons' quarters when Bess stepped out, her eyes searching his face. She stood very straight, the high, round breasts almost challenging, and he saw the pugnaciousness in her round face. "You all better?" he asked mildly.

"Better enough," she snapped.

"Better enough for what? Getting into more trouble?" he prodded.

"No, for being grateful," Bess said. "But I see you're being kept satisfied."

"You don't see anything. Your damn temper's in the way," he answered. "Thea's been a lot of help to me."

"I'll bet," Bess snapped tartly.

"You just naturally bitchy?" Fargo asked mildly.

"No, some people inspire me," she flung back, and spun into the shelter.

He chuckled as he swung onto the Ovaro and rode into the valley. She'd tried to make him feel guilty, and her ability to somehow be hurt and pugnacious at the same time made her very desirable. They were very different, she and Thea, he mused idly as he rode, physically and emotionally. Bess was all rounded, her sturdy little figure composed of rounded hips, full thighs, and high full breasts, whereas Thea was small and thin, yet terribly sinuous, her small breasts perfect for her litheness. The outsides and the insides fit each—Bess's quick temper all out in front and Thea's quiet, simmering steel. They had really only one thing in common: they were both very female. Mary Fuller swam into his thoughts and Nell Owens edged herself into the background. He'd have to be careful, he told himself. A man needed a little elbowroom to juggle.

He reached the end of the valley and urged the pinto into a canter, slowing to a walk when he neared Lansing's spread. The night had deepened and the ranch was dark as he reached the outskirts. He halted and slid from the horse, his eyes searching the corrals and the bunkhouse. He noticed a tiny glow near the bunkhouse—someone drawing on a cigarette. He looked down the length of the nearest corral and saw a dark figure leaning against the far corner fencepost. Lansing kept guards posted, he remembered. Perhaps it meant something, but perhaps not. Lansing was aware of the hostility of the valley people, so it'd be no more then prudent to keep sentries posted.

Fargo left the Ovaro under a red cedar and circled around the corrals to the back of the house, crouching as he surveyed the area for more guards. The two in front were the only ones in sight. He made his way toward the rear of the main house. He saw the storm-cellar door almost flat against the ground and carefully lifted one of the two doors. He stepped into the blackness of the few steps leading to the cellar and lowered the door after him. Groping with one hand against the wall, he inched down the steps. He came to another flight of stairs and climbed until he reached a door. He found the iron handle and opened the door to peer out. The living room took shape in front of him as the light from a lamp in the hallway provided more than enough illumination. He saw the heavy wooden desk and he made his way to it on footsteps soft as a mountain cat. The top drawers of the desk were locked with simple snap catches, and Fargo drew the thin blade of his throwing knife from its calf holster. He slid the blade back and forth along the latch of the first drawer until he found a spot where he could press the knife against the lock, and he felt the drawer snap open.

He unlocked the next one and the one below it before opening the first, and when he pulled the drawer open, he saw the neat, round stacks of money in the drawer. Dorrance Lansing kept a good supply of cash on hand. He rifled deeper into the drawer and found a collection of receipts for cattle sales. Pushing the drawer closed, he went on to the next one. It contained a ledger that listed expenses and income—mostly expenses, he observed. The third drawer held files and he eagerly brought them out only to feel his lips tighten with disappointment. The files held only personal letters, deeds to the property, an old will in which he saw the name Francis Lansing. He put the files back in place and rifled through the other open drawers of the desk, to end up cursing silently as he found nothing at all.

He let his glance move over the room. The desk was the only place logical for the man to keep claims or the copies. It was where he kept all the other papers important to him. He checked the drawers to make sure each was properly closed again, and left the room on silent footsteps to retrace his trail through the cellar and out the storm door. He crouched low as he returned to where he'd left his horse, the two guards still in place, he noted. He walked the Ovaro away from the outskirts of the ranch and mounted only when he'd put enough distance between himself and the ranch. He rode back through the valley under a moon that had begun to move toward the horizon, and he fought off frustration. True, he hadn't come up with a damn thing to help, no answer for anything yet, but maybe he was inching his way to the next answer he needed. He hadn't found what he went there looking to find. But maybe he'd found something else.

The thought crystallized as he reached the camp and rode to the far edge. He halted, unsaddled the Ovaro, and pulled his bedroll into the trees on the slope. All the exhaustion of the past two nights swept over him as if a dam had burst, and he slept heavily far into the dawn.

7

It was midmorning when he walked down the slope into the camp. Ruth Simmons still had coffee simmering over a low fire and a few good biscuits left, and he accepted both hungrily. When he finished, he started toward the Ovaro and saw Thea come toward him, her eyes searching his face.

"Expected you to stop by last night," she said, and he caught the reproof in her tone.

"Too tired to talk," he said.

She fell into step beside him as he went to the Ovaro and began to saddle the horse. "You find the claims?" she asked.

"No," he said.

"I told you you wouldn't," Thea said. "He's not bothering with that."

"Somebody's bothering with claims. Everything being legal and recorded wouldn't be so important otherwise," Fargo said.

"What do you mean by 'somebody'?" Thea frowned.

"I think we're chasing the wrong fox," he said, and saw her eyes grow wide.

"Just because you didn't find any land claims?" she scoffed.

"That's one thing. He's not the man he's supposed to be. He's more weak than strong. That's another. He didn't take the bait when he could have. That's still another. It spells something wrong," Fargo answered.

"You're reaching. Of course it's him. You know why he wants the land now," she said.

"I know why somebody wants it."

"It's got to be him. Every single thing that's been done to us has involved Dorrance Lansing. That's no coincidence," Thea said.

"No, it's not," Fargo agreed. "But things aren't always what they seem to be. Either we're chasing the wrong fox or he's got Judge Tolliver holding the claims for him. You keep saying he's clever and careful. I'll find out."

"How?"

"By paying Judge Tolliver's office a late-night visit," he said.

Thea's eyes became more gray than green and her hands closed around his arm as he put the latigo strap through the rigging ring. "You can't," she said. "It's too dangerous. You're a dead man if they catch you."

"If they catch me," Fargo said as he finished tightening the cinch and started to lead the pinto away.

"Don't do it, Fargo," Thea said.

"Got to. It's time for answers," he said.

Thea's mouth turned tight and she flung words out. "Be a fool," she said as she spun on her heel and strode away.

Fargo walked on, the Ovaro behind him. Bess appeared, her round face grave. "Couldn't help hearing the last part," she said. "Maybe you are being foolish."

"That's part of the game," he said. "But thanks for caring."

"Don't know why I bother, seeing as how that's all being taken care of," she said crossly.

"Every little bit helps." He smiled as he mounted up and rode from the camp. He rode unhurriedly through the valley, paused to let the horse drink and rest at a wandering stream that crossed his path. The day had slid into afternoon when he headed into Owl Creek. He slowed the horse to a walk. The courtroom and the judge's chambers were only a few doors from the sheriff's office and the jail, he remembered, and he neared the sheriff's office first. He frowned as he saw the men lined up outside the door to Roy Curry's office. He steered the Ovaro closer and paused. "What's happening?" he asked the last man in line.

"The sheriff's hiring twenty new deputies," the man said.

Fargo felt the frown dig deeper. That'd give the sheriff some twenty-five deputies all together, he estimated, about twenty-four more than he needed in Owl Creek. Fargo's lips drew back. Roy Curry was preparing for something. Whatever it was, Fargo muttered, he was damn sure he wouldn't like it. He started to move on when he heard the harsh voice behind him.

"You're a nervy bastard coming into Owl Creek, Fargo," the voice said, and he turned in the saddle to see the sheriff's small features pulled together in a half-snarl. Behind him, Judge Tolliver's spindly form looked on. "Strainer died," the sheriff said.

"Trying to find his nose?" Fargo asked.

"From loss of blood, you bastard," the sheriff roared.

"He must've been a hell of a deputy," Fargo commented, and Roy Curry frowned. "Seeing as how you're replacing him with twenty new men," Fargo explained.

"That's none of your damn business," the sheriff snarled. "The judge and I intend to keep law and order around here. I could have you clapped in jail right now and I might just do that."

"I don't think you'll do that," Fargo replied evenly.

"Why in hell not?" Roy Curry blustered.

"Well, you might sometime, but not this way with you standing out there in the open right in front of me. You know what'd happen." Fargo smiled.

"What's that?" Curry pressed.

"You know I'd put a bullet between your eyes before your boys even got their guns out of their holsters. You wouldn't want that, would you?" Fargo said through his smile. He flicked a glance at Judge Tolliver as he moved on and left Roy Curry to simmer in fury tempered by self-preservation. He rode casually down Main Street, but his eyes missed nothing as he passed the courtroom, the building old and almost ramshackle. He saw an ordinary lock on the front door and a narrow alleyway separating the structure from the one beside it. He rode on to the end of town and circled around to return along the back side of the street. He slowed as he reached the rear of the courtroom building and saw a flight of outside stairs that led to the second floor. Two barred windows flanked the stairs and he moved on, turned the horse, and trotted into the low hills west of the town.

He found a shade tree, a thick-branched hackberry, and he dismounted and lay down in the cool of its leafy cover. He catnapped as the day drew to a close, dozed again in the first hours of the night, and when he got to his feet, the moon was high in the sky. He led the Ovaro leisurely back to Owl Creek.

The town had grown still when he reached the edge of it, only the saloon an oasis of noise. He moved along the back of the buildings and dismounted when he reached the house with the steps up the rear wall. He tethered the Ovaro to a shadbush a half-dozen yards away and crept into the alleyway alongside the house. Moving silently, he edged his way to the front of the building. There was no guard, but he saw two deputies outside the jailhouse a few doors away. He slipped back down the alley until he reached the flight of stairs. He climbed the steps, testing each plank before putting weight on it. The second-floor door was locked, but he saw split, weathered wood at the edge of it. He grasped the doorknob in one big hand, turned with all the strength in his arms, and felt the old, half-rotted wood of the doorframe give way.

He pushed the door open and stepped into the blackness and let his eyes grow used to the dark. A sliver of moonlight crept through a single window to let him barely discern the stairway leading down. He moved to the steps, once again testing each one. He halted to listen when he reached the bottom, but he heard no sound coming from any of the other rooms in the house. Two first-floor windows allowed more moonlight in, and he found the makeshift courtroom and, behind it, Judge Tolliver's private chambers.

The smaller room was windowless and almost black. He saw a kerosene lamp in the larger room and his lips pulled back as he weighed the risk, but he decided he had no choice. The room was too dark to find anything, much less read what he found. He turned the lamp on and closed the door to the courtroom, grateful that the smaller room was windowless.

The lamp spread its soft glow outward to illuminate a small wooden desk and, in one corner of the room, a small iron safe. He decided to try the desk first and pulled the top drawers open, surprised that they were unlocked. The reason became plain quickly enough: he found the desk held only a collection of unimportant papers, legal stationery, forms, a territorial seal, and a half-dozen yellowed law journals. He turned to the safe. It was securely locked; he examined the solid iron handle and knelt down to peer at the underside. Its only weak spot was where it joined the door of the safe. Two or three heavy .45 slugs fired into the underside would probably blow the safe open where the handle and the inside bolt joined. But he didn't dare risk it. The shots would sure as hell bring company on the run.

But the safe held what he sought inside its thick, steel walls, he was certain. The more he stared at it, the more positive he became. He felt the certainty of it inside him as the safe sat in front of him, a silent, implacable challenge. He rose, tugged at it, managed to move it only a scant six inches. It would take three men to carry it. He'd have to return with help, he decided. He started to turn from the safe when he heard the sound of the front door being unlocked, followed by excited voices. "It's his horse, I tell you," he heard a voice say. "I'd know that Ovaro anywhere. I was passing back behind the buildings when I spotted it."

The sheriff's voice answered, barked orders. "Search the place, every damn crack. Get some light on," the man said.

Fargo blew the kerosene lamp out as the sounds of running feet moved into the building. Five, maybe six men, he guessed. He had maybe ten, fifteen seconds before they turned a lamp on. There was no time left for anything except to make a break for it. The Colt in hand, he slammed into the door and bolted out of the room. A cluster of shadowy figures moved through the darkness, and Fargo fired three shots and heard one cry of pain as the other shapes dropped down for cover. He spun and raced up the stairway.

"There he goes. Get him," Roy Curry shouted, but Fargo had reached the top of the stairs in three quick bounds. He streaked from the building and started down the outside flight of steps. He'd just reached bottom when he saw the two figures run out of the alleyway alongside the house. He fired and one figure fell while the second dived back into the alleyway.

Fargo raced for the Ovaro and vaulted onto the horse as other figures appeared, two racing from the building at the top of the outside steps. He heard their shots, the bullets far off mark, as he sent the Ovaro into a full gallop. But he heard Roy Curry screaming between oaths. "Get your horses. Get the new men. We're goin' after him," the sheriff ordered, and Fargo heard him bark one more command. "Somebody check the safe," Roy Curry said, and Fargo smiled as he rode into the night, the sheriff's words as much a confirmation as a precaution.

He turned the Ovaro and raced into the valley, straight through the center of the rich, soft land as the moon painted a pale path for him. The camp came awake as he galloped in with a shout and he saw the figures stumble from their tents in nightclothes. Bess stared at him, her eyes wide and full of concern, a short nightdress clinging to her high, round breasts, and he saw Thea appear in the long man's shirt, slender legs beautifully provocative. He stayed in the saddle, waited for the last to emerge, Nell Owens and Ted and Mary Fuller.

"The sheriff will come here looking for me," Fargo said.

"You find what you wanted?" Thea interrupted.

"Almost," he answered. "But I was interrupted. He'll have a fair-size posse with him. Let him search the place. I don't want any shoot-out. Let him search. It'll use up time and nobody gets hurt."

"Where will you be?" Thea asked.

"In Black Canyon. He won't be running me down up there. One man can hold off ten there," Fargo said. "But I want three men with me in case he does try to make a fight of it up there."

"Be right with you, Fargo," Ollie Joust said.

"Me, too," Kelby chimed in.

"I'll go," Ned Simmons volunteered, and ducked into his tent to dress.

Fargo found Thea's eyes as he waited. "Still think you're right about chasing the wrong fox?" she asked.

"So far," he answered, and wheeled the pinto as the three men approached with their horses. He saw Thea disappear into her tent as he started to ride off. Bess watched him go, her eyes wide, concern filling her round face.

He led the men to where Black Canyon rose up in craggy, towering shapes. He took the first path leading up and then veered off into a second narrow pass. He climbed steadily and glanced back at the three men following, Ollie Joust and Kelby nearest, Ned Simmons last.

"Single file from here," he called back as he guided the Ovaro along the narrow ledge that looked down into the chasm below. The moon lighted the black face of the rocks across the narrow gorge and the sound of the rushing water below echoed up the steep, narrow sides. He finally turned from the narrow ledge into another passage that opened onto a flat area surrounded by low craggy rock forms of black schist. They were halfway up into the heights of the canyon, almost as far up as where the silver was supposed to be buried. It was far enough, he decided. A quick glance around the rocks bounding the area showed only two pathways to the spot from below.

"This'll do," he said as he dismounted.

"You think Roy Curry's going to chase us all the way up here?" Kelby Joust asked.

"He could. He's afraid I might be onto something," Fargo said. "In any case, we ought to be able to hear them coming up the passages from here."

"Christ, we could hold an army off from here," Ollie

Joust said. "They'd have to come out those passageways almost one by one."

"We settle down and listen now," Fargo said, folding himself comfortably against a wall of black rock almost facing the nearest of the passages. The others settled themselves and silence surrounded the little circle of crags. Sound echoed up through the gorge, bounced back and forth across the black rock sides of the chasm. Fargo relaxed, confident they'd hear a posse on the way up long before it reached the high narrow passages.

He waited, almost relaxed as he heard the others stir, shift, move in place with nervous tension, and he smiled. Learning to wait, as the hawk and the red man wait, took years to master, and some men never did. He leaned his head back against the black rock and listened. Night in the rock crags of Black Canyon was a strangely still time, with none of the woodland night creatures to fill the dark with their sounds. He let his thoughts idle, turn to twenty new deputies. They'd been hired with something special in mind. There was something in the wind, Fargo thought, frowning. Were the planners getting nervous? Had Dorrance Lansing given orders to break up the camp at the valley's end? They'd need a good-sized force for that. But had Dorrance Lansing given orders at all, for anything?

Fargo was toying with the question when he heard a sound, the faint scrape of a boot heel on stone. Fargo cursed, pushed himself forward, and whirled to scan the tops of the crags. He saw a figure, a dark shape against the night sky, with a wide-brimmed hat and a rifle. He threw himself to one side as the shots rang out, the first two grazing the back of his legs. He heard the rest of the volley slam into the stones and glimpsed Ollie Joust and the others rolling along the rock walls for cover. He came up against a piece of stone, spun on his back, and whipped out the Colt. But the figure had disappeared, dropping down behind the top of the rocks.

Fargo leapt to his feet. "You two stay, cover the passages," he called to Ollie Joust and Simmons. "Kelby, you come with me."

He scurried up the side of the rock crags, catching hold of crevices and jutting edges and he heard Kelby Joust following. He halted at the top and saw the crag curve down in a slide that ended at a narrow ledge across the deep gorge. Kelby came up beside him.

"You take that end," he said as he scurried to the other side of the crags and let himself slide down the curving black rock. He reached the narrow ledge sooner than he'd expected, the gorge staring up at him, and he reached out, grasped a piece of stone, and clung to it as his arm cried out in protest. He drew his feet back from the edge of the narrow ledge, felt the deep rush of relief escape him as he stood up.

Kelby's voice cut into his moment. "This way, Fargo," Kelby shouted from the other end of the ledge, and Fargo began to run along the narrow pathway. He caught sight of Kelby Joust ahead, racing after the shadowed figure but being outrun. He peered past Kelby and decided he couldn't risk a shot at the distant figure. Bearing down, he started to draw closer, but the racing figure, barely visible, continued to stay ahead on the narrow ledge. Suddenly the distant figure turned and seemed to race in midair across the gorge.

"Rope bridge," he heard Kelby call back. "He won't get away."

Fargo saw the rope bridge come into sight, a single thin strand across the gorge with another single strand as a rail. The fleeing figure had reached the other side when he saw Kelby race onto the swaying strand. "Wait," he called, but Kelby had almost reached the center when Fargo saw the rope bridge tear loose at the nearest end.

As he watched in helpless horror, Fargo saw the thin strand sail through the air with what seemed agonizing slowness, the loose end flapping downward into the gorge. Kelby Joust screamed as his precarious grip tore away and Fargo felt his lips pull back as he watched the young man's body plummet into the gorge, his scream echoing up the narrow sides until it ended with shattering abruptness.

"Goddamn," Fargo swore softly, and felt his clenched fingers digging into his palms. He pulled his fists open and slowly walked to where the rope bridge had torn loose. The shredded ends remained embedded in the rock crevice where they had been secured. He stared at the shred of rope and turned his gaze to peer across the gorge at the opposite side. Thoughts tumbled through his mind, grim thoughts, angry ones, unanswered wonderings and thoughts as dark as the night. He turned away finally and found a place that let him climb back to the top of the crags and down to the flat area where Ollie Joust and Ned Simmons sat, guns in hand, their eyes still on the two passageways until they saw him appear. They had to have heard Kelby's scream and he saw the dread in Ollie's eyes. He recounted what had happened and saw Ollie fall silent and stare at the ground.

"I'll go look below for Kelby's body tomorrow," he said finally. "Nobody came up the passages."

"Nobody," Ned Simmons echoed. Fargo nodded, and Ned Simmons went on to say exactly what Fargo expected he'd say. "They got smart. They were afraid we'd hear them so they sent one man up alone." Fargo nodded again. It was the sensible explanation and he had nothing with which to reject it. Yet it stuck in his throat. "It might even have been Lansing himself. He knows the canyon," Simmons speculated.

"It wasn't Lansing," Fargo said. "And he doesn't know the canyon."

"Then one of Roy Curry's boys," Simmons said.

"Let's head back," Fargo said, and pulled himself onto the Ovaro. The others followed him down the twisting, narrow paths and along the edge of the chasm until they reached bottom. Darkness made picking up tracks impossible, but Fargo did see a pathway of broken brush ends that told him the sheriff and his posse had been there. He rode in silence back to the camp and he saw Charlie Burrows waiting on a stool. Ruth Simmons rushed from her tent, relief on her face when she saw her husband. Charlie had only to look at Ollie Joust's face to know the facts if not the details. The little man rose to his feet as Fargo halted and dismounted.

"They came, just as you said they would, Fargo," Charlie told him. "Roy ordered the camp searched. He was real mad when they didn't find you. They took off for Black Canyon in a hurry." He peered at Fargo. "They come at you there?" he questioned.

"More or less," Fargo said as he took his bedroll and walked up the slope outside camp. He undressed and lay awake for a spell. All the tumbling thoughts that had raced through him as he stood at the edge of the gorge came back again. He let them whirl through his mind, not that he could stop them if he'd wanted. The night had brought new questions instead of answers for the old. Maybe the final answer did not lay in the judge's safe, he pondered. He finally turned on his side and slept, the new day only hours away.

Bess was the first to meet him as he came down to the camp in the morning. "Been waiting," she said, almost a pout on her round face. "Got something to say."

"Let's hear it," Fargo waited.

"I heard about last night. I got you into this, but I don't want to see you get yourself killed," she said. "Seems you're taking damn-fool chances."

"Going to take some more," Fargo said. "No other way to get answers."

"Maybe we all ought to just go on. There's been enough dying," Bess said glumly.

He took her chin in his hand. "I don't plan on getting myself killed. I want to give you another chance to be grateful," he said. She stared up at him and he saw the mixture of emotions in her eyes: wanting, resentment, jealousy, and caring. "You just behave yourself and don't pull any more fool things," he told her, not ungently, and strode away. He brushed down the Ovaro with a quick rub of the curry and had begun to saddle up when Nell Owens paused beside him. He saw her eyes search his face, and he waited.

"Suppose I said no special favors?" the woman asked.

He smiled and his glance took in the heavy breasts that ballooned up under the white blouse she wore. "That'd put a different face on it," he said. "Is that what you're saying?"

"Yes," Nell Owens said without a flicker of hesitation.

"I'll try to find a time," Fargo said, and watched her walk away, full, ample figure yet firm-fleshed as a teenager. A lot of woman, he was sure. But she was so easy to see through. She was being so typically female, goals unchanging, only the approach redone. She'd simply changed the order of things because she was certain the favors would follow the fucking.

He laughed to himself, finished saddling the Ovaro, and saw Thea walking toward him, her sinuous body beautifully graceful. "Going out to try and get yourself killed again?" she asked tartly.

"Wasn't planning to." He smiled.

Thea pressed her hands against his chest and the sharpness vanished from the green-gray eyes. "You've earned a rest. Spend the day with me. We'll go off someplace," she said.

"Can't," he said.

Her frown was instant. "Why not?"

"Got to go fox hunting." He laughed, and her lips tightened as she drew back.

"Dammit, you're being stupid as well as stubborn. Dorrance is your fox," she said.

"So you keep telling me," he said, keeping his voice even.

"What does that mean?" Thea frowned.

"Maybe you've your own reasons for wanting me to prove it was Dorrance Lansing. Maybe it's more personal with you," he suggested.

"Everyone in the camp knows it's him, except you," Thea countered.

He shrugged as he swung onto the pinto. "Everyone could be right," he conceded. "Or they could be wrong. I aim to find out."

Thea spun on her heel and strode away, and he moved the horse through the camp and saw Abby Weeden watching, the little woman's eyes sharp with her own thoughts. He tossed a smile at her and received a nod in return, and he sent the pinto into a canter as he left the campground. He rode halfway into the valley before he turned the horse west. Getting into the judge's office would be a far different task now, he realized. There'd be guards posted, perhaps not too many, he hoped. They'd take precautions, but they'd really not expect he'd come back. They thought logically, and logic could lead one astray. But he'd need more than he brought with him last time. Quick and hard, no attempt at stealth this time. He kept the Ovaro pointing west toward Saddle Rock. Special jobs needed special tools and Saddle Rock seemed the likeliest place to pick up what he needed. Perhaps in more ways than one, he pondered as his eyes narrowed.

He sighted a spiral of dust behind him, slowed, and

watched its path. Some of Roy Curry's posse hoping to find him, he grunted. But they were moving in the wrong direction and he rode on unbothered. He found Saddle Rock as the day grew long, but the general store was still open and he hitched the horse outside it. JACK HARDY, PROPRIETOR, the sign on the window read, and he entered. Jack Hardy was a balding man in a white clerk's apron and a dyspeptic air about him. "Need some gunpowder, small sack," Fargo said.

"Don't carry much of it," Hardy muttered.

"Thea Manning sent me," Fargo said, and saw the storekeeper frown at him. "You know Thea Manning, I was told," Fargo said. The man shrugged as he continued to frown. "Small gal, black hair, nice-looking," Fargo said, and felt his own frown gather. "Comes in here every few weeks and loads up on supplies."

"Oh, her," the man recalled. "Yes, I know who she is."

"Understand you give her a special price," Fargo pushed.

Hardy's face turned a shade more dyspeptic. "You understand wrong, mister. Nobody gets a special price," he said.

"Guess I heard wrong." Fargo smiled. "Can I have my gunpowder?"

The storekeeper walked to the rear of his store and returned with a canvas sack he put on the counter. "That'll be five dollars," he said.

"Much obliged." Fargo nodded as he paid, and carried the gunpowder outside and tied it to his saddlebag. The little frown stayed on his forehead as he led the pinto away and walked slowly through the town. He carefully noted everything there was to see, and though it hardly took much time, Saddle Rock was more of a town than Owl Creek. When he'd finished, he mounted the pinto and rode from the town with new thoughts sorting themselves in his mind, some quickly fitting in with the old, others still waiting on the sidelines. When he'd finished, he felt the grimness that had draped itself around him, and night descended before he was halfway to the valley.

When he finally reached its lush greenness, he turned and headed for Owl Creek under a pale moon. He was almost at the outskirts of town when he saw the riders appear and he sent the Ovaro into a line of red cedars. He watched the horsemen pass, caught the glint of the badges they wore. Roy Curry's new deputies, he grunted, damn near all of them, he counted as they rode past. He watched them move on and wondered where they were going. But he couldn't stop to find out, much as the desire to do so pushed at him. He had other things to do, and he dismounted and led the Ovaro as close to the rear of the buildings in town as he dared.

He tethered the horse in a cluster of bullberries as he came abreast of the building he sought, and as he'd expected, it was under guard. He crept forward, crouched, darted between two structures nearby, and made his way to the edge of the street and peered along the face of the buildings. He saw the two guards at the front door and he retreated to the rear, where a single guard waited at the foot of the outside steps.

He crouched and touched the sack of gunpowder he'd taken from the saddlebag. With a length of lariat he'd cut, he made a fuse, tying one end of the rope to the neck of the sack of gunpowder. He had done his own dry run, counted off seconds, and he went through it again as he crouched within sight of the guard at the rear stairs. The fuse would give him fifteen seconds to take cover from the direct blast. The two guards in front would come storming in at once, but he'd made plans to give himself another thirty seconds at that end. All in all, he figured forty-five seconds to set the blast, take cover, let the gunpowder blow the safe door open, scoop out the contents of the safe, and run to where he'd left the Ovaro. Not a hell of a lot of time, he grunted grimly. He couldn't afford to stumble.

He half-rose, drew the double-edged throwing knife from its calf holster. The men he faced had orders to shoot to kill, and he felt little compunction about what he had to do. It was his neck or theirs, and he preferred it to be theirs. He drew his arm back, the thin blade poised, waited till the sentry shifted himself and presented a better target. The knife hurtled through the darkness and Fargo was on his feet, running after it as soon as the blade left his hand. He heard the half-gasped sound as the knife found its mark and he caught the guard's figure before the man hit the ground. He lowered the already silent form noiselessly to the ground and pulled the thin blade from the side of the man's neck where it had embedded itself to the hilt. He dried the blade clean and returned it to the calf holster and hurried up the stairway to the top. The door lock hadn't been repaired, and he let himself in, found the inside steps, and started down.

He listened with each step until he was satisfied they'd stationed no one inside the building. The fact bothered him, and he thought of the twenty deputies he'd seen riding through the night. Something was afoot and he suddenly felt uneasy. Maybe he had set things into motion ahead of schedule and he swore silently at the thought. Reaching the bottom of the steps, he hurried into the courtroom, where one window let him see the dark bulk of the two guards just outside the front door. He picked up one of the long wooden court benches and put it down a fraction of an inch from the door, lowering it inch by inch until it touched the floor in absolute silence. He took another bench, turned it on its back, and laid it atop the first one. Three chairs were placed against the benches in careful silence and he hurried on noiseless steps to the smaller room.

He speared the safe in the corner with a quick glance, knelt down beside it, and attached the canvas sack of gunpowder to the handle. The short lariat fuse trailed down and he lighted the end of the piece of rope, waited a precious second to be sure it was burning, and streaked for the adjoining room. He knelt against the wall, his head ducked down. He counted, swore as the piece of rope took three seconds longer than he'd planned it to burn. The explosion, when it erupted, sent plaster falling from the ceiling, loosened the wood laths of the wall, and tore a hole in the wall of the smaller room. Fargo leapt to his feet and raced for the other room as the two guards started to burst in through the front door. He heard their curses as they fell over the benches and chairs.

But he was in the other room, peering through the smoke and the darkness to see the safe door blown off. He reached into the small safe, yanked out a half-dozen file folders and large manila envelopes. He ran, clutching the material, some ten seconds behind schedule, and he heard the two guards as they finally pushed their way in past the furniture. He reached the top of the stairway and bolted outside, virtually flew down the outside steps and across the flat ground to the Ovaro. He heard a shot follow him as he leapt into the saddle and glanced back to see the two guards had reached the top of the rear stairs. He sent the Ovaro through the trees, slowed, and listened. No one came after him and he rode on with his brow furrowed. Something was wrong, he bit out again. They were plainly the only three of Roy Curry's men on the scene. The others, including Roy and the judge, were off someplace.

Fargo pushed the material he'd taken into his saddlebag until he found a quiet place in the forest. He dismounted there, lighted a taper, and sat down with the file folders and envelopes. He rifled through the material in the flickering light of the taper, and a grin of satisfaction moved across his face. He held one part of the answer in his hand, but now he knew there was another part. He finished going over the papers and blew the taper out.

Stuffing the material back into his saddlebag, he swung onto the Ovaro and headed for the valley and the campground. He rode with his eyes scanning the darkness as the moon bathed the night shapes in its pale light. He saw no signs of the sheriff's gang of deputies as he reached the valley, and the uneasiness pushed at him again. He sent the horse into a canter and finally saw the camp tents come into sight.

He rode into camp and saw Abby Weeden's small gray-haired figure standing in front of one of the tents. As he dismounted, he saw the tent flap open and the two Simmons youngsters came out followed by the Thompsons' little girl. His glance lifted to scan the other tents. No one came out, nothing moved, and a knot suddenly formed in his stomach. His eyes went back to Abby Weeden.

"They're all gone," the little old woman snapped, disgust in her voice.

"Gone where?" Fargo frowned as the knot tightened.

"To make Dorrance Lansing give them their lands back," Abby said.

"Why all of a sudden? What in hell brought that on?" Fargo asked. "What the hell got into them?"

"Judge Tolliver and the sheriff were here," Abby said. "They rode in together. The judge told everybody that he and the sheriff had found evidence that Lansing had railroaded everybody out of their lands. They apologized to everybody for what had happened."

"Shit," Fargo bit out.

"Just what I said to myself," the little old woman snapped.

"And they all went storming over to Lansing's place?" Fargo said.

"It was Roy Curry who told them they ought to go and face down Lansing," Abby said. "They hadn't enough hard proof on Lansing, he said, but if they could scare Lansing into admitting it, they'd clear everybody of all charges now against them. The judge agreed, and they apologized again and rode away."

"Why didn't you go with the others?" Fargo asked.

"Because I told them they were fools," Abby said. "So they left the youngsters here with me and went riding off, every last one of them, Charlie included, the old fool."

"Goddammit," Fargo said as he pulled himself onto the Ovaro and sent the horse charging off at a full gallop. The knot in his stomach was now a leaden ball. Some of the questions that had continued to jab at him were being answered, and he cursed Roy Curry and Judge Tolliver for their single-minded, ruthless cleverness. The details didn't matter, the outline was all too clear, and he raced the Ovaro up the slopes of the valley to cut time to Dorrance Lansing's place. He finally raced across the flatland that brought him in sight of the ranch. He saw the semicircle of horsemen first and then the other figures seated on the ground against a line of alders. He circled and came up on the other side of the trees and made his way through the thick cover. He dismounted as he reached the end of the alders.

He saw Nora and Fred Thompson, Ollie and Tad Joust beside them, and the others in a half-circle, each with their hands bound behind them. The sheriff's deputies faced them, guns trained on the helpless group. Fargo's eyes continued to move over the semicircle, picking out Mary Fuller, Nell Owens, and Ted Fuller. Charlie Burrows sat at the very edge of the trees, and as Fargo scanned the group again, he saw that Thea wasn't among them. He started to creep toward Charlie, moving along the grass on his stomach, pulling himself along on his elbows. He halted as he saw the sheriff and Judge Tolliver move forward on their horses to face their prisoners.

"Dorrance Lansing is dead, murdered inside his house, along with five of his men. The others ran for their lives, I presume," the judge intoned, his gaunt face grave. "Murder's murder, whether it's done by one man or a gang. I find you all guilty of murder and sentence you to be hung at sundown tomorrow."

"Why wait that long, you lyin' bastard?" Fargo heard Fred Thompson call.

The sheriff answered. "Practical problem," he said. "We've only got one gallows and it'll take too damn long to hang you all one at a time. We'll have to find us four or five good trees close together so we can hang pretty near everybody at once."

He had answered with the calm and reasonable logic of a man discussing how to best fence in a piece of pastureland.

Fargo had to force himself not to draw the Colt and blast Roy Curry's square head into smithereens. But it wasn't time for that yet, and his mind raced as he saw the sheriff turn to Judge Tolliver. Their plans might be speeded up when they learned their safe had been blown open. "You take two of the men and get back to town. I'll stay here and see to getting this bunch back without trouble," Fargo heard the sheriff say to Judge Tolliver as he inched closer, almost to Charlie's back.

"Don't move," he whispered, and saw the little man's back straighten. "Talk to me without turning your fool head." He flicked a glance at the center of the semicircle, where the judge had started to ride away, three of the deputies going along with him. "What happened?" he whispered.

"Lansing and his men were dead when we got here," Charlie said. "We went into the house and there they were. Before we could turn around, that whole passel of Roy Curry's men surrounded us."

"You did just what he wanted you to do, all of you come racing over here," Fargo said. "You were all so greedy to get your land back, you took the bait like a starving trout takes a worm."

"On your feet," Fargo heard the sheriff order.

"Don't tell any of the others I was here," Fargo said. "What happened to Thea?"

"She came with us. She must've slipped away somehow," Charlie Burrows whispered as he pushed himself to his feet.

Fargo slid backward in the grass, stayed on his stomach, and watched the deputies fall in beside their prisoners. He glimpsed Bess, her round, pugnacious face angry. He lay still until the procession faded into the dark. Another question had been answered, he realized as he rose to his feet and returned to the Ovaro. The night was nearing its end when he rode back to the valley. Morning was spreading itself across the sky when he reached the camp. Abby Weeden sat in front of the tent where the children were sleeping, and as he halted, he saw Thea's tent flap open. Thea rushed from it, her eyes wide as she hurried toward him.

"I know," he said, and she slowed, frowned at him. "I was there, got a chance to talk to Charlie." Thea halted as her eyes searched his face.

"Is he all right?" Abby cut in.

"He's a prisoner, like the others," Fargo said. "How'd you get away?" he asked Thea.

"I ran out a side door of the house as Roy Curry's men

came," Thea said. "I hid in the trees until I got a chance to get away. I was lucky."

"I'd say so," Fargo said as he sank down on a piece of log and pulled the Ovaro around to stand beside him. "It all fits now," he said almost sadly. "Every last rotten piece of it."

8

Thea stared at him, waiting.

"Dorrance Lansing was never behind any of it," Fargo said. "That ought to be plain enough now. I didn't find any claims at his place because he never filed any, never had any intention of it."

Abby's voice cut in. "Then why was he involved in everything that happened to us?"

"Roy Curry and the judge engineered it to look that way. They set him up as the villain each time. They knew you'd all see him as the one to blame, and the way they handled it, it sure seemed that way. Poor Lansing never knew how he was being used. They planned it perfectly, right down to the last move."

"Which was?" Thea asked.

"The reason they let you all stay camped together," he answered. "They had plans for you—taking the blame for killing Lansing. They knew how everyone would jump at the chance to face him down, which is exactly what everyone did. Their apology was a perfect touch. You all took the bait and rushed to Lansing and they were ready and waiting for you. It tied everything up neatly and they figured to add Lansing's land to the rest."

"The wrong fox," Thea murmured.

"Very wrong," Fargo said, and reached up into the saddlebag. He pulled the file folders from the safe and waved them at Thea as Abby looked on. "Claims filled out and ready to file for every piece of land in the name of Sheriff Roy Curry and Judge Samuel Tolliver. They were waiting to wrap everything up before filing. I just pushed them into moving ahead of their schedule."

Abby Weeden's voice cut in. "They haven't got their claims now. You have them. But they can still hang everybody and file new ones," she said.

Fargo rose and pushed the file folders back into his saddlebag. "Won't do them much good," he commented. "Lansing wasn't the only one being used."

Thea frowned and her green-gray eyes peered hard at him. "What does that mean?" she questioned.

Fargo's smile was wry. "If they ever file these claims, they'll find every piece of land already has a claim filed on it," he said. "In the name of Thea Manning." His wry smile stayed as he met Thea's stare.

"You gone crazy?" she asked.

"Like a fox," he answered. "Want me to spell it out?"

"Please do. This should be amusing," Thea said through narrowed eyes.

Fargo's smile vanished. "I don't think you'll find it that," he said. "You knew Dorrance Lansing wasn't strong enough or ruthless enough to pull off all the things that were happening. You were really the only one who knew it besides Roy Curry and the judge, until I became sure of it. When you realized what Roy and the judge were doing, you saw your chance. You let them go on, set up each incident while you quietly beat them at their own game."

"Then why did I rush off to Lansing's with everyone else just now?" she countered.

"You couldn't have very well hung back, not after how you'd been one of those who accused Lansing the most. You had to carry on your little charade," Fargo said. "But you knew Roy Curry and the judge were lying. You knew they were planning something and you were ready to slip away before it happened."

Fargo watched Thea half-turn from him. He saw her hand touch her blouse and stared at the small rimfire lady's pistol she'd drawn from inside the shirt. Four shots only, he saw, European-made, but at this range well able to kill. Thea's green-gray eyes had become almost all gray. "Take your gun out, slowly," she ordered. He obeyed, saw her hand stayed steady. "Throw it over there," she said, and he tossed the Colt across the ground. "How did you know?" Thea asked.

"I didn't, not till that night in Black Canyon when the rope bridge broke under Kelby Joust's weight. Only someone very light could have made it across. That let out any of Roy Curry's posse, and no one else except those in camp knew where I'd be. It let out all the men in camp, too."

"I wasn't the only woman there," Thea said.

"No, but it has to be somebody not only light but somebody quick, with a body able to move like a cat. Now, that didn't fit Nell Owens, Nora Thompson, Bess, or anybody but you," he said.

"You were guessing," Thea said.

"Some," he admitted. "But I was getting damn sure. My visit to Saddle Rock clinched it. Jack Hardy didn't know you except as a customer. He was no special friend giving you a special price."

"You've been busy," Thea half-smiled, and Fargo saw the pistol continued to hold steady.

"Know what else I found in Saddle Rock?" Fargo said. "A mail-coach service that runs back East every week. You volunteered to get supplies, not because you got a special price. That was an excuse to let you make regular trips to the mail stage. You could file a claim every time somebody new lost their land."

"Damn you, Fargo. Why didn't you just listen to me?" Thea said.

"I did, until you tried to blow my head off in Black Canyon. That kind of thing annoys me," he said, and cast her a curious glance. "I figure you were going to wait till Roy Curry and the judge finished with everybody else and then take care of them yourself," he said.

"That's exactly what I'm going to do," Thea said. Fargo nodded and stared into space for a moment. "What are you thinking?" she asked.

"Who's worse, those two or you?" he answered. "I don't guess there's much to choose."

"You won't have to think about it for long," she snapped, and he saw her eyes flick to Abby Weeden, who stared almost in shock. "Into the tent with the kids," she ordered. "Come out and they're dead along with you."

Abby blinked and backed into the tent.

Fargo's eyes bored into Thea. He had to break her self-assurance, make her shoot the little pistol in anger. He had to make her flare up, explode, and be ready for it. All he needed was a split second, but her icy calm denied him. "You're a real fourteen-karat bitch," he said. "You know you're going to have to kill Abby. She heard everything."

"You won't have to worry about that, either," Thea said.

"I should've known you were a goddamn phony when I had you in the sack," he said, and saw her green-gray eyes flash.

"You bastard. There was nothing phony then," she snapped.

"There was nothing good about it, either," he said, half-laughing.

"Son of a bitch," Thea flung back. "You enjoyed it."

"Crazy wild's one thing. Good's another," he pushed, his eyes riveted on her hand with the gun.

"Goddamn bastard," Thea almost screamed. He saw her raise the little pistol, her finger start to tighten on the trigger. He dived, slammed into her knees, and felt the heat of the shot across the top of his head. She went down, the second shot going wild into the air. He brought one big fist around and slammed it into her stomach.

"Aaaagh," Thea gasped as the breath rushed from her and she drew her knees up in pain.

He saw the little pistol fall from her hand as she rolled onto her back, her face contorted. He rose, kicked the pistol into a bush, and retrieved his Colt.

"You . . . you bastard," Thea managed as she held one hand to her stomach.

"You bitch," he returned, and reached down, yanked her to her feet with one hand. Half-dragging her to the Ovaro, he took a length of lariat and tied her wrists first, then her ankles, and flung her to the ground. Her breath had returned and hate pushed pain aside in her eyes. "Abby," he called. "Get out here."

The tent opened and the little woman appeared, her eyes wide with surprise. "Leave her there and keep an eye on her," Fargo said harshly. "If she tries anything, bash her head in with whatever's handy." He turned and pulled himself onto the Ovaro.

"What are you going to do?" Abby asked, and he saw three little heads peering out from the tent. "Or maybe I ought to ask what can you do?" she said.

"Going to bargain some. They don't know about Thea, but they know I've got their claims. They'll want them back," Fargo said. "They release everybody and I'll give them their claims."

"You think those liars will stick to a bargain?" Abby asked in surprise.

"No, I know they won't. But I'm going to let them

think I believe them," Fargo said. "While I'm gone, you round up every rifle in camp."

"All right," Abby said, and he sent the Ovaro into a gallop. He rode hard through the valley, uncertain exactly how Roy Curry and the judge would react to finding their claims gone. He counted on a period of indecision on their part as they tried to decide the best course. They'd consider bargaining, he reasoned, knowing all the time they'd no intention of keeping any bargain they made. When he neared the end of the valley, he halted beneath a thick hackberry, removed the file folders of claims from his saddlebag, and pushed them deep into the underbrush. He swung onto the horse at once and headed for Owl Creek.

When he reached town, he rode directly to the sheriff's office and took note of the line of horses tethered across the street, most of the deputies gathered nearby. He saw jaws drop and brows lift in astonishment as he halted, swung to the ground, and walked into Sheriff Curry's office. Judge Tolliver was with the sheriff, along with two deputies, and he saw both men stare at him in disbelief. Roy Curry recovered first and spoke to the two deputies. "Leave us alone," he said, and closed the door after the two men. He turned back to stare at the big black-haired man in front of him. Judge Tolliver's gaunt jaw still hung open, Fargo saw. "You are either the stupidest or the nerviest bastard I've ever seen," the sheriff said.

"Maybe some of both." Fargo smiled. "But I've something you want and you've something I want. I figure it's a Mexican standoff."

"You got the claims with you?" the sheriff said, his eyes narrowing.

"I'm not that stupid," Fargo said.

"Search his saddlebag," he barked.

Judge Tolliver hurried outside but returned in moments. "Nothing," he said.

"You want to deal?" Fargo asked calmly. "You let everybody go and I'll give you your claims back. You'll have everything the way it was, except for holding everyone for a murder you committed. But there's nobody going to prove that, anyway."

"Bring the claims and we'll let them go," the sheriff said, his little features crushed together in the center of his square head.

Fargo laughed. "We exchange, but not here. You bring the prisoners and I'll have your claims," he said.

"Where?" Roy Curry growled.

"The beginning of Black Canyon, the first line of rocks," Fargo said. "I'll be waiting there."

"What if I say no deal? What if I just take you in now?" the sheriff asked shrewdly.

"I'd kill you first, and you know it," Fargo said. "You don't deal and I take the claims and the whole story to Washington myself. You don't have everybody. Thea Manning's still free. So's Abby Weeden."

He watched the sheriff exchange a quick glance with Judge Tolliver. "The first line of rocks at Black Canyon," Roy Curry said.

"One hour before sundown," Fargo said. "No tricks."

"No tricks," the man said, and Fargo strode from the office with the grim smile held inside him. Neither of them knew how to spell honesty, he grunted as he swung onto the Ovaro and rode from town. He headed back to the campground, riding hard. The sun moved too quickly through the noon sky and he reached the camp to see Thea on the ground, her eyes glaring hate at him, Abby seated on a wooden chair and a pile of rifles beside her, more than enough for every man and woman held prisoner.

"Went through everybody's belongings," the little woman said.

"Good work," Fargo said as he dismounted, found a piece of canvas, wrapped the rifles in the cloth, and placed them on the front of his saddle. He yanked Thea to her feet. "Get the youngsters," he told Abby. "The sheriff will be passing through here on his way to Black Canyon. I don't want anybody here. I'm going to put you up on one of the slopes." The woman shepherded the three children, put them onto one horse, and brought her own mount around.

Fargo sat Thea in front of him on the Ovaro and led the way from the camp. He rode up a slope not too far away but well hidden, and deposited everyone in a glen of alders, swinging Thea to the ground. "Keep watch on her," he warned Abby, and the woman nodded.

Thea's eyes were almost all gray. "I'm going to kill you, Fargo," she said with quiet ice.

"You tried that twice," he threw back harshly. "One more and you're out." He turned to Abby. "Somebody will come by for you later. Might even send Charlie."

"He better come ready to apologize to me," the little old woman snapped, and Fargo chuckled as he rode away, the rifles in the sack balanced in front of him. The sun was in the midafternoon sky when he reached the first line of rocks that marked the beginning of Black Canyon. He rode through one of the openings between them to the flat space behind, and he dismounted, unwrapped the cache of rifles, and put the guns on the ground. Riding back in front of the line of rocks, he halted and let himself relax in the saddle. The sun's hurried path told him it wouldn't be a long wait, and before it reached the edge of the high crags of the canyon, he saw the parade of horses approach. He waited, one hand on the butt of the .45 at his hip.

Roy Curry and the judge were in the lead, the prisoners behind them shepherded by some twenty deputies, he guessed. The sheriff halted a few feet from him, and the rest of the procession came to a stop. "The claims," the sheriff growled.

Fargo's eyes swept the sheriff's prisoners, pausing at each one until he was certain they were all there. He paused for a moment longer at Bess and saw her pert face was still full of anger and pugnaciousness. "First let them go," he said to Roy Curry. The man hesitated. "You've got twenty men ready to cut me down if I don't give you the claims," he said. "I just want to make sure you keep your end of the deal first."

The sheriff shrugged and another quick glance exchanged between him and the judge. "You've a suspicious nature, Fargo." Roy Curry shrugged and called back to his men. "Let them go," he said.

Fargo moved his horse back at the mouth of the nearest opening through the line of rocks and watched the captives move single file toward him. Fred Thompson was first, his eyes apologetic as they met the big man's hard stare. Fargo spoke through lips that hardly moved.

"Behind the rocks," he said. "Get ready." He saw Fred Thompson frown, but he knew the man would understand the minute he saw the rifles. The others followed through the opening and Fargo let himself appear to be counting. When the last one had gone through the opening to disappear behind the line of rocks, he turned the Ovaro and moved to where Roy Curry and the judge waited. He had retrieved the file folders from the underbrush where he'd hidden them and he reached into his saddlebag and handed them to the judge. He waited as the judge scanned through them quickly, saw his gaunt face almost smile.

"Everything's here," he said to the sheriff.

"A deal's a deal," Fargo said cheerfully.

"Sure, a deal's a deal," Roy Curry said, and it took an effort for him not to snarl the words, Fargo saw. He watched as Roy Curry and the judge rode back to where the twenty deputies were halted, and he saw the sheriff rein up, turn, and shout to the men. "Get in behind those rocks and kill every one of those bastards," Roy Curry said. "It'll be like shooting sitting ducks. They haven't got a peashooter among them."

Fargo heard the men's shout of glee as they charged forward, and he turned the Ovaro through the opening and raced behind the line of rocks. His eyes swept the scene. Everyone had a rifle waiting, poised steady against the far wall of rock. He leapt from the Ovaro and yanked the big Sharps from its holster at the same time. He was flattened against the first line of rocks when Curry's men burst through the openings in the rocks. The explosion of gunfire resounded up the canyon and he watched Curry's men topple like ninepins as, completely taken by surprise, they raced in to be cut down from all sides. He saw one try to wheel his horse and escape, and he ended the attempt with a single shot from the Sharps.

Flinging himself onto the Ovaro, Fargo raced back through the opening. Roy Curry and Judge Tolliver were on their horses, staring back at the line of rocks, faces wreathed in frowns as they became aware that something was wrong, the explosion of rifle fire and shouts more than they expected.

Their frowns turned to panic as they saw the big man on the Ovaro charging from behind the rocks toward them. "Goddamn," Fargo heard Roy Curry curse as he whipped his horse into a gallop. Judge Tolliver fell in behind him, both men streaking for the trees. The Ovaro closed the distance quickly, and Fargo saw Roy Curry swerve to the right and send his horse crashing through a thicket of barberries.

Judge Tolliver swerved in the other direction, and

Fargo slowed the Ovaro, brought the big Sharps to his shoulder. He fired, and Judge Samuel Tolliver flew from his horse, his black frock coattails flapping in the wind as though he were a wounded crow. He hit the ground, tried to get up and run, but fell, and Fargo reined the Ovaro to a halt. The judge half-turned and Fargo saw him draw an old Walker Colt from inside his frock coat. His gaunt face already seemed a death mask as he raised the gun to fire. Fargo's shot turned the mask into reality and the judge hurtled backward, collapsed onto his back, and quivered for a few moments as his black coat turned red.

Fargo heard the sound of Roy Curry's horse crashing through the underbrush and he wheeled the Ovaro to chase after the man. Terror held the sheriff in its grip and he made no effort to hide his flight. Fargo followed the sound until he could glimpse the man ahead of him. He sent the Ovaro full out and Roy Curry turned in the saddle to see the big horse racing headlong through the trees after him, not unlike a black-and-white avenging angel. He skidded his horse to a halt, turned, and yanked his six-gun from its holster. He fired, emptied the gun at the onrushing figure, and Fargo dropped flat in the saddle, his face against the Ovaro's neck alongside the powerful trapezius muscle, as the shots whistled past him. He half-rose in the saddle, saw Roy Curry reloading, and he raised the rifle. He fired and Roy Curry's chest caved in as he spurted blood and bits of bone. Fargo reined up as the man fell from his horse, lifeless before he hit the ground.

"A deal's a deal, you bastard," Fargo said quietly. He turned the Ovaro and slowly rode back to the canyon. The others were there waiting in front of the line of rocks. Ted Fuller had a superficial shoulder wound, he saw, and Ruth Simmons wore a bandage on one arm.

Fred Thompson spoke for all as Fargo halted before them.

"We don't have the words for thanking you enough," he said. "We should've waited for you. We did it all wrong."

"You did," Fargo agreed, and his glance swept their faces. He saw contrition, apology, even shame, written on each except for one, Bess Hanford. Her pugnacious little nose wrinkled and she met his gaze without flinching.

"A mistake's a mistake," she said.

He shook his head. "Seems you're trying to corner the market," he said, and her lips tightened as she turned her eyes from him. He swung the Ovaro around. "Let's get back to camp. There's more you don't know about. I'll explain on the way."

He told them about Thea as they rode. They listened in shocked silence, and when they reached the camp, Bess came up alongside him. "Guess I'm not the only one who makes mistakes," she said smugly.

"I find out about mine before it's too late," he returned, and spoke to Charlie Burrows. "Abby is up on the first long slope, inside a thick stand of alders," he said.

"Know the place," the little man said.

"Fetch her and the youngsters back. Put a halter on Thea and let her walk behind your horse," he said.

Charlie nodded and cantered away.

Fargo dismounted. He felt Bess watching him, but he paid her no attention.

Nell Owens paused beside him. "That offer still stands, Fargo," the woman said. "No reason to turn it down anymore."

"No reason at all." He grinned, and Nell walked on. He let his glance go to Bess. "You waiting for something?" he asked cheerfully.

"No, absolutely not. Most definitely not," she flung at him, and whirled away. He sat down and Ned Simmons appeared with a bottle of whiskey.

"Thanks," Fargo said as he took a long draw.

"Figured you could use it," the man said. He sat down beside Fargo. "It's not done with yet. Thea Manning's filed claims on all our lands. Maybe she won't give them up," he thought aloud.

"False claims," Fargo said. "She knew what Roy Curry and the judge were doing. She's no right to those claims. The claims office will see that." Fargo gazed out across the valley and the frown dug into his brow as he spotted the lone horseman racing toward the camp. The figure became Charlie Burrows and the little man skidded his horse to a halt, fought for breath as he gasped out words.

"Thea . . . she got loose," he said. "She's got a gun. She has Abby and the youngsters. She says she'll kill all of them unless you come, Fargo. She wants you, alone, without a gun."

The others had come up at once, and Fargo met their stricken faces as he remembered Thea Manning's promise. "My kids," Ned Simmons said. "And Fred's. But we can't ask you to do any more, Fargo. We'll go. Maybe she'll listen to us."

"Not a chance," Fargo grunted bitterly. "She wants her revenge, and that's me. You even try getting near her and she'll kill your children."

"My God," he heard Mary Fuller breathe. His glance swept the others, fastened on Tad Joust.

"You're built most like me," he said as he started to pull his jacket off. "Take my jacket, my shirt, and my hat," he said. "I'll take your horse and you ride the Ovaro."

"What're you going to do?" Fred Thompson asked.

"Try to circle around behind her while she's watching Tad come up the slope," Fargo said, and handed the younger man his clothes. "Charlie will leave you at the bottom of the slope. Keep your head down and move slowly up toward her. She'll see the Ovaro, my hat, and my jacket. She'll be looking to see that my holster's empty. You'll be just about up to her before she'll see it's not me." He handed Tad Joust the Ovaro's reins and swung up on the man's brown gelding. "Remember, keep your head down, the hat shading your face," he said as he raced away. He streaked toward the long slope and veered sharply off to his left before he reached out to send the horse climbing up a steep side of the valley. When he reached the top, he turned again and rode south. He was above the alders now, he knew, and when he came to the top of the long slope, he turned the horse downward but only for a few dozen yards before he dismounted.

He moved down the slope silent as a cougar, peering through the thick tree cover until he saw the alders. He slowed as he began to dart from tree to tree. He spotted the figures just below him, Thea with one of the youngsters, Abby and the other two children frozen in fear to one side. His eyes narrowed and he swore silently as he saw Thea had the barrel of the gun against the child's head. He moved down a half-dozen yards closer and halted. He wanted all her concentration on the horseman coming up the slope, and he had only a few minutes to wait before he saw the Ovaro moving up slowly. Thea shifted position, rose onto one knee, but he saw she pressed the end of the gun barrel into the child's temple. She had her other arm pulling the youngster in close, and he swore again.

If she moved or he missed, he could kill the youngster. But the Ovaro was growing closer. Tad Joust still seemed the figure of the man she waited to kill, but the improvised masquerade was close to ending. When it did, her fury would be boundless. Thea Manning was insane with rage and hate, totally consumed. She'd shoot the child she held instantly, maybe Tad next or Abby and the other two children. Fargo rose to his feet and unholstered the Colt. He moved down the slope and saw Thea peering hard at the approaching Ovaro and its rider. There were only seconds left. He had made her react once in haste. He had to do so again. She had to pull the gun from the child's temple. He took another step, raised the big Colt .45, and took aim.

"Waiting for me?" he asked.

He heard her hiss as she spun around, her reaction instant and automatic. The gun barrel dropped from the youngster's temple and Fargo fired as Thea Manning turned to him. He had time only to see the surprise and the hate in the green-gray eyes as the heavy .45 slug sent her small figure crashing backward down the slope. She kept rolling until she slammed against a tree, and for a moment her legs moved, twisted, writhed sinuously, and he turned away. She was still when he looked back, and she seemed to resemble a broken doll.

A long breath escaped him and he saw Tad standing with Abby, the three youngsters clinging to them both. For the first time he saw the little woman had a red bruise on her temple. "What happened? How'd she get loose?" he asked.

"She asked for some water. I had one of the youngsters bring the canteen to her. She got her arms up and grabbed him by the throat. She told me to cut her loose or she'd choke him to death, and she was doing it right in front of me. She'd a death grip on him. I had a skinning knife in my bag and I cut her loose. She took the knife from me and knocked me down and found the gun in my saddlebag."

"Not your fault," Fargo said. "Things go wrong sometimes. Go back with Tad. I'll be along."

He waited as they made their way down the slope, Tad taking his own horse, and when he was alone, he pulled a collection of loose branches together. He made a bower over her and covered the branches with leaves. Pity, not sorrow governed his actions, he decided as he finally rode the Ovaro down into the valley as the dusk came.

The women were starting cooking fires as Fargo rode in. Tad and Abby had told them everything, and he sat down beside one of the fires. He forced himself to have some of the warmed beef jerky Nora Thompson gave him. "What happens now?" Charlie Burrows asked.

"She had no blood kin. I'll sign an affidavit of what took place here, and you can all claim your lands back," Fargo told them.

"What about that silver Lansing was so sure was buried up in Black Canyon? Think there's a chance it's there?" Ned Simmons asked.

He shrugged. "You want to come up with me in the morning and stand guard for the Utes, I'll give it one more try," he said.

"Why not?" Ollie Joust said. "We divide it if we find it."

"See you, come morning," Fargo said as he rose, stretched, and took his bedroll from the saddle. He started across the camp to the far edge and saw Bess moving toward him. She halted as Mary Fuller stepped from her tent. "I'm ready for that second time, Fargo, whenever you are," she said in a demure voice that didn't match her words.

He nodded. "I'll remember that," he said.

"Please. Soon," Mary said, and stepped back into her tent.

He let his eyes move out to where Bess had halted. "You waiting for something again?" he asked innocently.

"No, absolutely not. For the very last time, absolutely not," she bit out. "Why don't you give out numbers?" she flung at him as she whirled and strode away.

He walked on, the smile lacing his mouth. He found a spot, bedded down, and welcomed the quiet peace of deep slumber.

9

The morning dawned dark, with rain pelting down. "Want to call it off?" Fred Thompson asked.

"No," Fargo said. "Might be a good time. The rain might keep the Utes away." He took all the men with him as he rode from camp. Bess determinedly looked the other way as he passed her. The rain came down harder as they reached Black Canyon and he led the way up through passageways that ran deep with water. The journey took longer than usual as the rain continued to come down hard, and it was past noon when they reached the place where he'd dug into the hard red clay. He halted and stared at the spot. The hard red clay was no longer hard. The heavy downpour had softened it and Fargo watched as it oozed down the spiral and slid over the edge of the rocks to drop into the gorge below. He heard the laugh as it welled up inside him.

"There's your silver," he said as the others frowned. "Lansing and his map were probably right . . . once. It was buried there years and years ago, and years and years of heavy rains washed it all down into the gorge with the red clay. That's why nobody could find it. Nobody ever will."

He looked up at the sky and saw the rain beginning to lessen and the faint glow of sun fighting its way through the gray. He saw something else on the high crags above them, a line of near-naked horsemen that halted to look down at them. "Damn," he heard Ollie Joust say. The Utes stayed motionless, each man holding a bow in hand. "They can rain arrows down on us," Ollie muttered.

Fargo's eyes searched the line of braves on the edge of the high crags. "They could, but they're not," he said. "Move slow and follow me." He walked the Ovaro into one of the narrow passageways. There was no room to find cover if the Utes decided to shower them with arrows, but he moved slowly downward, turned into another pass.

"They're letting us get out of their canyon," Ollie said.

"Got to be a reason," Fargo muttered as he continued to lead the way down. The passage turned, emerged onto the narrow ledge that bordered the chasm below, and he saw the lone horseman blocking his way. He glanced up and saw the line of Indians watching from above. He halted and the others reined up behind him on the narrow ledge.

"What's he doing there all by himself?" Ollie asked. "Holding us up so the others can make porcupines out of us here on this damned ledge?"

"They could've done that already," Fargo said, his eyes on the Indian in front of him. "I told you there had to be a reason. He's it. He's the one that ran the other day. They're giving him a chance to redeem himself."

"On us?" Ollie asked.

"On me. He has to beat me, man to man, here on this ledge," Fargo said, and he swung carefully from the Ovaro, found just enough room on the ledge to put his foot down.

"Put a bullet through him," Fred Thompson called out.

"They'll put a hundred arrows in us, then," Fargo said. "We'll have cheated him out of his right to redeem himself."

"Shit," Ollie said. "If you lose?"

"I lose, you all lose," Fargo said. "I win and I'm pretty sure they'll let us ride out of the canyon this time." Fargo saw the Ute swing from his pony, and he moved toward the Indian. His eyes narrowed as he peered at the Ute. There was hate in the Indian's black eyes, but there was fear, too. He had fled death once. He didn't relish this second chance at dying. The Ute was plainly not filled with the tribal code of death before all else. Given his chance, he'd probably run again, but he had no chance this time. His chiefs had seen to that. But fear makes for desperation, and Fargo knew he faced a desperate man driven by fear and survival.

He moved toward the Ute and saw the Indian go into a half-crouch, digging powerful legs firmly into the earth. The ledge was but a stone ribbon, and below it, instant death. Fargo realized that he was too big to do battle on the ledge. It was a place for a small, wiry man, and the Ute fitted that description.

Fargo moved forward again another step and watched the Indian's leg muscles. He was but a scant foot from the Ute now and the Indian feinted with a blow that drew no response. The Indian half-spun and kicked, and Fargo pulled back as the moccasined foot grazed his abdomen. The Ute wanted to close for hand-to-hand combat, but Fargo backed away. The Ute may have decided that redemption included taking his enemy over the gorge with him. His eyes stayed on the man's legs, saw the muscles twitch, and ducked away from a round-house kick. Again the Ute came in and Fargo backed, and this time the Indian grew bolder as he half-twisted and kicked. But Fargo's eyes had stayed on the man's leg muscles and he was ready for the blow. He reached out, got one arm around the Ute's calf, and yanked. The Indian crashed to the ledge, landed on his buttocks, one leg half over the edge.

Fargo drove a hard kick into the man's ribs, and the Indian grunted in pain, rolled away, and leapt to his feet as Fargo went after him. Fargo saw the wildness in the man's black eyes, he saw the Indian gather thigh muscles. He dropped to the floor of the ledge as the Ute sprang at him. The Indian's body slammed into him and he fell back against the one wall of the ledge. He felt the Ute's hand grab for his shirt, and he drew his knee up, dug it into the Indian's abdomen, and lifted. He heard the man's scream as he fell sideways over the edge of the ledge, the scream trailing off into nothingness at the bottom of the gorge.

Fargo pushed himself to his feet, using the wall of rock at his back for support. His glance lifted to the line of figures atop the high crags. They remained motionless, as still as the rocks beside them. He felt the line of perspiration trickling down his chest as he carefully pulled himself onto the Ovaro and proceeded slowly along the ledge. A passage led downward where the ledge ended and he steered the horse through it. When he reached a lower place where the high-walled passage ended, he looked up, sought the line of figures above. They were gone. "We're home free," he said to the others. Nobody cheered and they finally reached the bottom of the canyon, that line of rocks that had been so important only a day ago.

The sun came out brightly when they reached the campground and Fargo saw that two of the tents had been taken down and that others were being dismantled. "No reason we can't move back to our lands," Ned Simmons said. "It'll take months for all the legal stuff to be done with."

"No reason I know of," Fargo said in agreement, and

he saw Bess loading things onto her brown mare. "You going back, too?" he asked.

"Yes," she said. "Pa will hear about what happened in time and he'll come back. No concern of yours, though."

"Took your advice," Fargo drawled, and she frowned in question. "Handed out numbers," he said. "Yours had number one on it." Her eyes stayed on him, searched his face. "Unless you're not interested any longer."

"I'm interested," she said quickly. "Damn you, I'm interested."

"Race you to your place," he said, and laughed as she slipped trying to leap onto the brown mare. He watched her race off and saw Charlie and Abby watching, a few of the others behind them. He waved to them as he swung onto the Ovaro and rode away. He didn't hurry and let Bess go out of sight. When he reached the cabin, he saw the door ajar and he pushed his way inside.

She had folded herself on the long green sofa, wearing only a pair of pink bloomers. Her round breasts pressed up, her firm, chunky little body overflowing with energy. But her face still held its pugnaciousness. "You have to promise to answer me something afterward," she said.

"Whatever," he agreed as he shed clothes. It was no time to think about questions and answers.

Bess lifted her arms as he shed the last of his clothes. She flung herself against him, all vibrant wanting and firm-fleshed energy, a chunky bundle of desire. No sinuous, twisting, lithe writhings for Bess, and he found himself glad for that. He drank in her simple, earthy, pumping energy, all the direct, unvarnished enjoyment of flesh upon flesh, outer and inner sensations merging to become one, and when she exploded with him, he held her round body hard against him until finally she fell back. He waited as she drew in deep drafts of air.

He lay beside her and enjoyed the bustling beauty that

was hers. She pushed herself onto one elbow, one high breast resting lightly against his chest. "You promised you'd answer," she said, almost a pout in her voice. He nodded, waited. "Why me? Why not the others? They were waiting, offering," she said.

"I started with you. Thought I ought to end with you." He grinned.

"I want an honest answer," Bess protested. "Why me? I'm not all that much more beautiful."

He took her face in his hands. "Beauty's not all outside," he said. "Nell Owens wanted to make up for a mistake. Mary Fuller wanted another try at growing up. You wanted for no reason except wanting. That's its own kind of beauty."

She leaned her firm breasts against his chest. "I know another reason," she murmured. "Fate."

"Of course. Slipped my mind," he said. He leaned back and pulled Bess with him. He could stand a few weeks of this kind of fate, he muttered silently.

Looking Forward

**The following is the opening section
from the next novel in the exciting
Trailsman Series from Signet:**

The Trailsman #38

THE LOST PATROL

---

*Snake River country, 1861, a dark and
bloody land, where a Bannock war chief and
prophet has united his people in a campaign to
wipe out the settlers pouring through this country . . .*

It was the time of yellow leaves, high in Snake River country.

Skye Fargo stood knee-deep in swift, icy water, his narrowed eyes peering into the timber on the far shore not twenty yards distant. A moment before, he had seen a shadow moving through the timber and, on peering closer, had caught the gleam of proud antlers. With his Sharps at the ready, Fargo waited for the big buck to push through the thick growth on the riverbank and lower its head to drink.

Fargo was taller than six feet, with broad, powerful shoulders. From under his gray, broad-brimmed hat, a thick pelt of raven-black hair reached almost to his shoulders. His massive chest swelled his deerskin jacket and his arms resembled small tree trunks. Keen and wide-set, his eyes were lake blue, his nose a powerful blade that dominated his craggy eaglelike countenance.

The chill from the icy water burned into his thighs. Already the wind from Canada was making the nights cold, whereas the heat at midday had him peeling off his jacket and mopping his brow. But the air in this high country was as sharp and clean as a newly stropped razor, and Fargo always felt good up here, even when it meant a white man had to keep a tight grip on his scalp and sleep with his Colt handy.

He had spent most of the summer searching the small mining towns along the eastern flanks of the Rockies for sign of two men a sheriff had described to him. The two men had proved elusive, but when Fargo finally caught up to them, he found only a couple of ragged, lice-ridden no-accounts who had never been south of the Snake.

On the opposite shore, the leaves of an aspen trembled slightly, even though the air was perfectly still. Fargo raised his rifle. Abruptly, an antlered head thrust out through the branches. It was a big buck with magnificent, large brown eyes and broad black snout. The buck raised its head to test the air, but Fargo was downwind and his rigid figure standing in the shallow water could have been a rotting stump. The elk looked directly at Fargo, then stepped out into the stream and lowered its snout to the swift water. Fargo had a clear shot. But he was forced to lift the Sharps' barrel slightly. That movement was all it took. With one bound, the wapiti vanished back into the brush.

Without bothering to bemoan his luck, Fargo turned and waded ashore. He was a patient man who from the very beginning had never expected anything to come easily. And it never had.

He climbed through heavy timber toward a distant ridge. Reaching it at last, he paused to look back down the slope and caught the glint of blue water through the trees. For a fleeting moment an indefinable sadness fell over the big man. Sometime, somewhere—the exact time and place lost forever in the crowd of years past—he must have looked down a similar slope, his small hand held in his father's large, comforting paw, the wind, like now, sighing through the pine branches high above his head.

Fargo shook off the feeling, turned, and kept going. He was not a sad or a melancholy man, and he seldom found himself reliving the past, except when it gave him the impetus he needed to finish the grim task he had set for himself so many years before.

Traversing the ridge, he kept on and plunged down a forested slope. He moved easily through the fragrant, shadowed world, his stride long, his steps as soft as a whisper on the needle-packed ground. His mount, a powerful black-and-white Ovaro, he had left at Will Cuppy's cabin on the banks of the Feather River. Will Cuppy still trapped beaver in these mountains and Fargo was on his way to check out the traps he and Will had set the day before. The bottom had long since fallen out of the beaver market, but Will had a buyer on the Oregon coast who still shipped sizable cargoes of beaver pelts to Brazil and Argentina.

Fargo reached the bank of a quiet stream and followed it until he came to a thick growth of riverbank willows, where Will kept his eight-foot-long dugout canoe. Stepping into the canoe, Fargo pushed away from the bank, then drifted silently downstream. The late-afternoon sunlight brushed with gold the tops of the willows and cottonwoods along the banks. Fargo crouched alertly in the canoe, aware of every movement in the tall grasses lining the shores, his lake-blue eyes studying the shoreline, searching for the sets he and Will had put down.

At sign of the first trap, Fargo nudged the canoe into the bank. Dropping his Sharps and gun belt into the bottom of the canoe, he stripped off his buckskin shirt and slipped into the icy water. The trap was set underwater at the shoreline, a tender willow shoot placed above it in the open just above the water, the end dipped in castoreum, the beaver's glandular secretion used to bait the traps.

The trap held a mature young male. On approaching the baited willow stick, the beaver had stepped onto the pan of the trap as it lifted its nose to the bait. When the jaws of the trap snapped shut on its leg, it had panicked and dived for deeper water, dragging the trap with it. The trap, chained to a stake driven into the muddy bottom, had held—and the beaver had drowned in the deep water near the middle of the stream.

Fargo dumped the carcass into the dugout, made a long cut down the belly of the dead animal and crosscuts down each leg. Then he chopped off all four feet and stripped the pelt from the carcass, using the bowie to scrape off adhering bits of flesh and fat. Except for the succulent beaver tail, he tossed the carcass into the brush along the shoreline.

The second trap had been set nearby. Before he reached it, Fargo saw the float stick tugging in the gentle current. This one also had plunged for the middle of the stream, its thrashings uprooting the stake holding the chain. The weight of the trap and the six-foot length of chain had pulled the beaver down all the same, and it had drowned. The floating stake told Fargo precisely where to look.

After skinning this one, Fargo tossed the bloody carcass alongside the other one and climbed back into the dugout. The remaining three traps had been placed a quarter-mile farther down the stream on the other side. But his luck had not been so good here. One trap was untouched. In another trap the jaws had closed on a foot, but the animal had managed to gnaw off its foot and escape. In the third trap he found a mangled youngster who had struggled ashore, only to become an easy prey for a predator.

The sun was low now, the chill deepening. Paddling back up the stream, Fargo nosed the canoe into the same willow thicket where he had found it. He jumped into the shallows and grabbed hold of the prow to haul the canoe deeper into the willows.

That was when he sensed danger.

Dropping the canoe, he whirled in time to see the gray, humped neck of a battle-scarred old grizzly rising out of the willow sprouts. One side of its muzzle had been shot away and the eye socket above it was empty. Hanging from its bloody snout were the bloody remnants of the two carcasses Fargo had only recently tossed into the willows farther down.

The huge grizzly was after its dessert.

Snarling furiously, the grizzly splashed toward Fargo. All Fargo had on his person to defend himself was his knife. He would sooner attack the grizzly with a willow switch. Dodging back around behind the canoe, he reached in for his gun belt and the Sharps. The grizzly grabbed at the canoe and flung it aside. As the hollowed-out cottonwood log slapped back down onto the stream's surface, Fargo charged through the willows and up onto the bank. The grizzly flung itself about and followed.

Fargo could almost feel the ground shaking under him as the grizzly clambered up the embankment and followed into the trees after Fargo. Desperately, Fargo turned and ducked aside just as the brute swung a taloned paw. Four razor-sharp claws raked Fargo's left shoulder. Landing on his back in the deep grass, Fargo dropped his rifle and drew the Colt from its holster. As the bear reared over him, Fargo thumb-cocked and fired. The round nicked the grizzly in its right side. With a shattering roar, the animal rocked back, and for an instant Fargo glimpsed its red tongue, its old ground-down teeth.

Then—incredibly—the old rogue spun aside and plunged off toward a clump of alders. It had already known the punishing fury of firearms, and Fargo's shot had reminded it once again of its lingering, crippling pain. But as the enraged animal vanished into the trees, it paused and looked back at Fargo. And in that single, malevolent glance, Fargo saw not a threat—but a promise.

Fargo got rockily to his feet, returned to the stream, and hauled the canoe back into the willows.

Once he had securely cached it, he inspected his shoulder. The grizzly's claws had left bloody tracks, and the skin had been laid back as neatly as if a surgeon's scalpel had been used. But no serious damage had been done. He washed the blood off in the stream, after which he slipped back into his buckskin shirt and jacket.

He took up the beaver pelts and tucked them securely under his belt. Then he grabbed his Sharps and took after the grizzly. He wanted to bring down this old rogue before it got the chance to surprise Fargo a second time.

The grizzly, a newcomer to the valley, promised to be a dangerous and troublesome one as well. For close to half a mile, Fargo followed the big animal's spoor before reluctantly giving up.

He was close to a familiar canyon by this time, and since it offered a more direct way to Will's cabin, he continued on toward it. He had almost reached the canyon when he heard the dim rattle of gunfire just ahead of him. Crouching low, he slipped cautiously through the timber until he reached a brush-covered ledge high above the canyon floor.

Peering through the brush, he saw a troop of cavalry doing its best to hold off a large Bannock war party. Fargo spotted the Bannocks in among the rocks and on the slopes overlooking the troopers. Three of the troopers, bandaged crudely, were lying out of action off to one side under the cover of a rocky overhang. The rest of the troopers were pretty well hidden.

The firing from both sides was steady but desultory. It looked as if the Bannocks were perfectly willing to wait out the troopers. The patrol was trapped with its back to the canyon's south wall. Well out of reach was their only source of water, the stream that cut through the canyon.

Fargo was not surprised to see this action. He had been expecting it.

For more than a year now the Bannock chief and prophet, Pashico, had been stirring up the Shoshone of the region, uniting them against the encroaching white settlers. And if Will Cuppy's information was accurate, Pashico had recently gained influence over Washakie's eastern Shoshone as well. The Bannocks in this war party below Fargo were obviously eager to bring back to Pashico's camp fresh bluecoat scalps and thereby win over to their cause still more Shoshone braves.

Picking his way carefully down through the brush, Fargo circled around behind the Bannocks until he found a trail of sorts that led down onto a small ledge that projected out over the canyon. Where the ledge joined the slope, a couple of pines were clinging to the canyon wall. Crouching down behind them, Fargo checked his Sharps, placed a handful of linen cartridges on the ground beside him, then pulled down the trigger guard and slipped a cartridge into the breech. Closing the trigger guard, he slipped off the safety and sighted on a Bannock in plain sight behind a boulder, his back to Fargo.

Squeezing off his shot, he saw the Bannock slam forward, then topple down the slope. Reloading swiftly, Fargo sighted on another Bannock farther down. The Indian had turned and was looking in Fargo's direction when the round blew a hole in his chest. Fargo got the third Bannock as he was scrambling frantically for cover up the steep slope. The troopers came alive. An officer led four or five men from cover, their revolvers blazing as they charged after the demoralized war party. Watching from the ridge, Fargo held up, his job done.

A few minutes later, he moved back off the ledge and picked his way down the steep slope to the canyon floor. The second lieutenant in charge of the patrol was waiting for him. As Fargo got closer, he noticed a bloody bandage under his hat. The officer could not have been much more than twenty-two or -three, a fair-haired, hazel-eyed youngster probably fresh out of West Point.

As Fargo approached, the lieutenant's beardless face broke into a broad smile. Behind him, a burly sergeant started over, his beefy face showing the relief he felt. Fargo shook the lieutenant's small-boned hand and found the grip surprisingly strong.

"I must say, that Sharps of yours was a most welcome sound," the lieutenant said. "My name's Tyler. Tim Tyler. And this here is Sergeant Jim Bradley."

"Sure glad you could make the party, mister," said the sergeant heartily, shaking Fargo's hand.

Fargo introduced himself, then asked, "What in blazes are you troopers doin' this deep in the mountains?"

"A wagon train set out for Oregon Territory," the lieutenant replied. "The wagon master had an agreement with Washakie that the Shoshone would not bother it, but after they pulled out, Washakie sent word to the fort that a number of his young bucks had joined Pashico's Bannocks and that he could not be held responsible. We were on our way to overtake the wagon train and escort it back to Fort Boynton when we were attacked by that Bannock war party."

"And so far," said the sergeant, "we ain't found no trace of that wagon train."

"Mr. Fargo," said the lieutenant, "do you have any idea how far we are from Lander's Cutoff?"

"Hell, that'd be about twenty miles south of here, I'd say."

The sergeant and the lieutenant exchanged glances. Then the sergeant looked at Fargo. "Guess we're lookin' in the wrong apple barrel," he admitted ruefully.

"I must take the blame," insisted the lieutenant. "On my advice, we took the wrong fork yesterday morning. This is certainly rough country."

"Very rough," admitted Fargo.

"At least we found the Bannocks," the sergeant commented ruefully.

"Mr. Fargo," said the lieutenant, "you seem to know this country well enough. Could I enlist your aid as a scout? It seems we need it."

"Sorry, Lieutenant. But if all you want is the cutoff, just go straight south until you hit the Snake. You should make it by this time tomorrow. Good luck."

"Thank you, Mr. Fargo," the lieutenant replied, obviously disappointed.

As the lieutenant and the sergeant turned and walked back to their men, Fargo watched them a moment, shaking his head slightly. The lieutenant appeared to be completely out of his element in this wilderness. It was only Fargo's fortuitous appearance that had saved his troopers from that Bannock war party. The Indians had caught the lieutenant with his britches down and had been all set to eat him alive. He and his patrol would have vanished without a trace.

Fargo moved back into the timber, climbed to the canyon's rim, then moved on until he had left the canyon far behind him. The lieutenant, he knew, would find it exceedingly difficult to head due south in this country, slashed as it was with ravines and wild, brush-filled gorges, most of them containing swift mountain streams that could pluck a man from his horse in an instant.

Fargo doubted the lieutenant would ever find that wagon train. But that was the army's business, not his. He and Will were busy enough just surviving in these mountains without messing with the army. Besides, he didn't like all these settlers coming in any more than the Bannocks or Shoshone did. They scared away the game and dirtied the streams.

With great, ground-devouring strides, Fargo kept on through the timber, his eyes alert for the pass he knew was somewhere ahead of him. At last he caught sight of it through the trees—a sudden open splash of sky. He kept on through a file of white pine, a timbered slope lifting skyward on his left, a deep drop-off showing through the trees on his right. Two chipmunks fled across his trail, tails straight up.

Instantly, Fargo flung up his Sharps and slipped off the safety. A Bannock, his face hideous in war paint, rushed him from the juniper cover. From behind Fargo came the swift pat of running moccasined feet. Fargo fired at the Bannock ahead of him. The round caught the redskin in his thigh and flung him to the ground. Fargo whirled and swung the barrel at an onrushing savage, catching him on the side of the head. A third Bannock caught Fargo a glancing blow on the side of the head with his tomahawk, but Fargo barely felt it as he shook it off and dashed to his right into a thick clump of junipers and plunged through them.

He almost stepped off into space.

Far below him he glimpsed a stream cutting through a heavily wooded gorge. He pulled up, but the moss-covered shelf of rock beneath his feet gave way and slipped over the edge into the gorge. Fargo slammed to the ground and reached for a bush to grab as he slid closer to the edge. He heard a Bannock breaking through the heavy cover of junipers behind him—and ducked. The lunging brave kept on going and plunged, screaming, into space. Fargo, scrabbling awkwardly in an attempt to arrest his slide, had to let go of his Sharps. It vanished beneath him.

As Fargo slipped over the edge, he glanced up in time to see the faces of three Bannocks staring down at him. For a moment he was airborne, then he smashed against a thick bush. He managed to grab hold of it for a moment. But the bush did not hold. Again he felt himself falling. He struck a pine poking out between a split boulder and flipped around it, then continued falling.

Twice the sky and the mountainside exchanged places. A boulder slammed into his back. The force of it knocked the breath out of him. But he remained wedged against the boulder long enough to enable him to grab hold of it and hang on.

His senses cleared and he looked up. He found he could no longer see the ledge he had fallen from—or the Bannocks. He looked down at the tops of pines far, far below him. Carefully, painfully—he wondered why he hadn't broken every bone in his body—he pulled himself along the face of the nearly perpendicular slope, moving from sapling to shrub to boulder until at last he found a narrow ledge that offered his feet a more secure purchase.

From there he was able to work his way a hundred feet or so lower, at which point he caught sight of a small rocky projection just ahead of him and, directly under it, what looked like a shallow cave. He reached it and took cover, pushing himself into the cave feetfirst. He heard a low growl and felt his right foot strike something soft and yielding. It felt like the limb of an animal, a large, fur-bearing animal.

He turned slowly and found he was sharing this small, denlike cave with a large male timber wolf. The wolf's snout was inches from his own. The wolf's lips curled back, baring its yellow fangs, and the low growl that emanated from deep within its throat caused the hair to rise on the back of Fargo's neck. For a mind-numbing instant Fargo felt the same primal terror that, from the beginning of time, must have struck any human confronted by these same bared fangs.

Then the fear left him. For a long moment he calmly met the wolf's gaze, feeling only a bone-deep weariness.

The wolf's snarl faded. Lowering its head to its fore-paws, it moved back an inch or two. Fargo turned back around, closed his eyes, and waited for night to cloak the mountains.

JOIN THE *TRAILSMAN* READERS' PANEL

Help us bring you more of the books you like by filling out this survey and mailing it in today.

1. Book Title: _____

   Book #: _____

2. Using the scale below, how would you rate this book on the following features? Please write in one rating from 0-10 for each feature in the spaces provided.

POOR		NOT SO GOOD			O.K.			GOOD		EXCEL-LENT
0	1	2	3	4	5	6	7	8	9	10

                                                RATING

Overall opinion of book .... _____

Plot/Story .... _____

Setting/Location .... _____

Writing Style .... _____

Character Development .... _____

Conclusion/Ending .... _____

Scene on Front Cover .... _____

3. About how many western books do you buy for yourself each month? _____

4. How would you classify yourself as a reader of westerns? I am a ( ) light ( ) medium ( ) heavy reader.

5. What is your education?
   ( ) High School (or less) ( ) 4 yrs. college
   ( ) 2 yrs. college ( ) Post Graduate

6. Age _____ 7. Sex: ( ) Male ( ) Female

Please Print Name_____

Address_____

City _____ State _____ Zip _____

Phone # ( )_____

Thank you. Please send to New American Library, Research Dept., 1633 Broadway, New York, NY 10019.

Wild Westerns by Warren T. Longtree

		(0451)
]	RUFF JUSTICE #1: SUDDEN THUNDER	(110285—$2.50)*
]	RUFF JUSTICE #2: NIGHT OF THE APACHE	(110293—$2.50)*
]	RUFF JUSTICE #3: BLOOD ON THE MOON	(112256—$2.50)*
]	RUFF JUSTICE #4: WIDOW CREEK	(114221—$2.50)*
]	RUFF JUSTICE #5: VALLEY OF GOLDEN TOMBS	(115635—$2.50)*
]	RUFF JUSTICE #6: THE SPIRIT WOMAN WAR	(117832—$2.50)*
]	RUFF JUSTICE #7: DARK ANGEL RIDING	(118820—$2.50)*
]	RUFF JUSTICE #8: THE DEATH OF IRON HORSE	(121449—$2.50)*
]	RUFF JUSTICE #9: WINDWOLF	(122828—$2.50)*
]	RUFF JUSTICE #10: SHOSHONE RUN	(123883—$2.50)*
]	RUFF JUSTICE #11: COMANCHE PEAK	(124901—$2.50)*
]	RUFF JUSTICE #12: PETTICOAT EXPRESS	(127765—$2.50)*
]	RUFF JUSTICE #13: POWER LODE	(128788—$2.50)*
]	RUFF JUSTICE #14: THE STONE WARRIORS	(129733—$2.50)*
]	RUFF JUSTICE #15: CHEYENNE MOON	(131177—$2.50)*
]	RUFF JUSTICE #16: HIGH VENGEANCE	(132009—$2.50)*
]	RUFF JUSTICE #17: DRUM ROLL	(132815—$2.50)*

*Price is $2.95 in Canada

**Buy them at your local
bookstore or use coupon
on next page for ordering.**

SIGNET Brand Westerns You'll Enjoy

(0451)

- [ ] LUKE SUTTON: OUTLAW by Leo P. Kelley. (115228—$1.95)*
- [ ] LUKE SUTTON: GUNFIGHTER by Leo P. Kelley. (122836—$2.25)*
- [ ] LUKE SUTTON: INDIAN FIGHTER by Leo P. Kelley. (124553—$2.25)*
- [ ] LUKE SUTTON: AVENGER by Leo P. Kelley. (128796—$2.25)*
- [ ] AMBUSCADE by Frank O'Rourke. (094905—$1.75)*
- [ ] BANDOLEER CROSSING by Frank O'Rourke. (111370—$1.75
- [ ] THE BIG FIFTY by Frank O'Rourke. (111419—$1.75
- [ ] THE BRAVADOS by Frank O'Rourke. (114663—$1.95)*
- [ ] THE LAST CHANCE by Frank O'Rourke. (115643—$1.95)*
- [ ] LATIGO by Frank O'Rourke. (111362—$1.75
- [ ] THE PROFESSIONALS by Frank O'Rourke. (113527—$1.95)*
- [ ] SEGUNDO by Frank O'Rourke. (117816—$2.25)*
- [ ] VIOLENCE AT SUNDOWN by Frank O'Rourke. (111346—$1.95
- [ ] COLD RIVER by William Judson. (123085—$2.50
- [ ] THE HALF-BREED by Mick Clumpner. (112814—$1.95)*
- [ ] MASSACRE AT THE GORGE by Mick Clumpner. (117433—$1.95)
- [ ] BROKEN LANCE by Frank Gruber. (113535—$1.95)*
- [ ] QUANTRELL'S RAIDERS by Frank Gruber. (097351—$1.95)
- [ ] TOWN TAMER by Frank Gruber. (110838—$1.95)*

*Prices slightly higher in Canada